5.1/7

D1308055

Escape!

"The north end is clean!" shouted one of the soldiers.

"Divide the remainder," Braddock replied. "Someone get a scanner down here. The device she's carrying will give her away."

A soldier passed within a dozen feet of Harley's hiding place. She ducked down quickly, then slowly raised her head again. She saw something different on the far wall—something that might be her only chance.

One of the windows of the building had been removed. In its place was the mouth of a huge yellow plastic pipe.

Harley looked at the open mouth of the pipe for the space of two heartbeats. Either it was going to lead her to safety, or to death. After what she had experienced, there was no way she was going to let herself be captured by Unit 17.

Harley rose to her feet.

"There!" shouted a soldier. "She's over there."

A scream came boiling from Harley's mouth. It wasn't a cry of fear, it was a shout of anger and frustration and defiance. It started in her stomach, gained force in her chest, and roared through her throat in a raw banshee wail.

Still screaming, Harley ran across the room and dived headfirst into the pipe.

Don't miss any books in this thrilling new series:

EXTREME ZONE

#1 Night Terrors
#2 Dark Lies
#3 Unseen Powers
#4 Deadly Secrets

Available from ARCHWAY Paperbacks

EXTREME ZONE

DEADLY
SECRETS

M.C. SUMNER

AN ARCHWAY PAPERBACK *Original*

An Archway Paperback published by
POCKET BOOKS, a division of Simon & Schuster Inc.
1230 Avenue of the Americas, New York, NY 10020

Produced by Daniel Weiss Associates, Inc., New York

ISBN: 0-671-00244-9

First Archway Paperback printing April 1997

10 9 8 7 6 5 4 3 2 1

Cold wind whistled through the alley, carrying off sheets of yellowed newspaper and forming miniature cyclones between the rows of trash cans. An old man pushed his shopping cart slowly through the chill breeze. He wore a threadbare army coat that had faded to the color of dust and a shapeless gray hat. His fingers, black with grime, stuck out of his tattered cloth gloves. The wheels of his cart squeaked with every grinding turn.

As the man reached the mouth of the alley, two women dressed in heavy winter coats passed along the sidewalk. The older of the pair glared at the man with disgust, but the younger woman's face showed more compassion. She reached into the pocket of her coat and came out with a crumpled dollar.

"Here," she said, thrusting out the bill as she passed the man.

The old man took the dollar and nodded. "Thanks, miss," he said in a rough voice. "Bless you."

As the women walked on, the old man chuckled to himself and tossed the dollar away. The swirling wind carried it over parked cars and lifted the green bill up into the gray winter sky.

After a quick glance in either direction, the man stuck his hand into the pocket of his worn coat to find a small, flat black cellular phone. He flipped it open to reveal an array of buttons and dials of incredible complexity. After quickly pressing a series of buttons, he held the small device up to his ear. The man heard a high trilling noise, then a loud click.

"Yes?" answered a buzzing voice from the tiny phone.

"Any sign of them up north?" asked the man in the filthy coat. His words steamed in the cold air.

"Negative, Commander," replied the voice. "We've got men in place all around the perimeter, but there's nothing to report so far."

"South?"

"No," said a different voice. "I don't . . ." There was a moment of silence. "Wait a minute. Commander, take a look at sector A-sixteen. There's something going on down there."

The man quickly wheeled his cart back into the alley. He fished among the rags and empty soda cans in the basket and pulled out a glossy metal device the same size and shape as a paperback book. With a quick tap of one dirty finger, the front of the gadget began to glow. The metal surface turned milky, then clear. Pale blue lines appeared in the air above the device. They wove around each other, snaking over and under, until they had formed a cube of glowing light. Within the cube, small forms took shape.

"SATELLITE 238C," read the glowing white text at the corner of the screen. "Sector A." With a second tap of the man's finger, the image within the cube grew in size. Gray squares turned into city blocks as the detail became clearer. Miniature buildings rose within the lines of light, separated by moving streaks of minute vehicles. A finer mesh appeared, dividing the cube again into three dozen smaller sectors. One of the blocks pulsed with crimson light.

The man frowned, his salt-and-pepper eyebrows knitting together above his slate gray eyes. He snatched up the tiny phone and held it close to his mouth. "What the devil is that?" he snarled.

"It looks like theta band activity," replied the crackly voice over the phone.

"Theta band? At a level you can detect over the satellite?" The man shook his head. "Impossible. It takes our best instruments to pick up theta radiation."

"That's what I'm reading from here."

The man put his hand into the glowing cube and touched the blinking spot. The image swelled again, until he could see distinct cars on the streets and space between the buildings. The spot of color moved along with one of the tiny vehicles. It was surrounded by a swarm of flickering, constantly shifting red numbers.

"It does appear to be theta activity," the man admitted. He rubbed one grimy finger along his iron gray mustache and grumbled under his breath, "And at a very high level."

"Do you think the energy is coming from the girl?" asked the voice over the phone.

"No," the man replied immediately. "This level of activity is well beyond anything we've seen. It's far too high to be generated by any individual." He slid his finger across the gadget, and the image zoomed in again until the numbers 10,000:1 appeared at the top of the screen. The picture was no longer as crisp as it had been. Details were lost in blocks of black and gray. But at this setting, the man could see that the vehicle was a large truck—and that it wasn't the truck that generated the red glow. The pulses of energy came from something so small that even at maximum magnification it was nothing but a single point in the three-dimensional display. And that point blazed with a silent crimson fury.

"A device," the man whispered under his breath. "She's got some kind of device."

"Are you sure it's Davisidaro?" asked a new voice over the phone.

The man snorted a cloud of steam into the cold air. The cloud drifted through the glowing cube, making the image waver. "Of course it's the girl." He stared at the miniature scene for a moment, then nodded to himself. "All right, here's what we're going to do. Pull in all the men on the north side. Have them set up a moving perimeter and follow. No contact at this time."

"But wouldn't it be better to apprehend them now?" asked the deep voice.

"No. I want to see where they're going."

"What if they get away?"

The man's lips turned up in a snarl. "If they get away, every man in the detail will meet a swift and painful end. Is that clear enough?"

"Yes, Commander," the voice on the phone replied quickly.

"Good." The man watched the truck move slowly through the cube, and the sneer on his face gradually turned into a smile. He reached through the hovering holo-gram and touched the flat screen underneath. Immediately the image dissolved in a flurry of multicolored sparks.

The man shoved the device that had produced the

display back into the battered shopping cart. "It appears that Ms. Davisidaro has found an instrument that may be strong enough to power her father's little experiment," he said into the phone. "We'll follow until we're sure we have all her companions. Then we'll move in."

"Yes, Commander."

"Then get on it. This is a priority-one situation. Get as many additional men as you need."

The old man slapped the phone closed and dropped it into the basket of rags. He reached deep under the pile of trash and came up with another device. This one was larger than the phone, with a contoured handgrip on one end and narrow muzzle projecting from the other. The man raised it slowly, smiling as his fingers closed around the grip.

He heard a rattling from down the alley. A pointed snout peeked out from among a stack of trash bags, followed by glistening eyes and a sleek gray body. The rat stepped out of the garbage and started across the alley.

The man whirled around and sighted down the barrel of his new device. The rat seemed to sense sudden danger. It scurried away quickly, its feet scratching against the cold ground. But it wasn't fast enough.

There was a high, whistling noise and a brief squeal. Then silence. The rat fell still. Fresh blood steamed in the cold.

"We'll catch them," the man breathed into the frosty air. He lowered his weapon and looked at the dead rat with satisfaction. "And once we complete the experiment, there will be no more need for Ms. Davisidaro."

The man smiled.

ONE

Noah Templer fell backward as a huge boulder tore free from the ceiling of the cave and came plummeting toward the earth.

The rock struck the cave floor with a noise like a thousand peals of thunder crushed into one bone-rattling roar. Splinters of shattered stone slashed against Noah's face, drawing thin streams of blood from his forehead, cheeks, and neck. He whirled around, looking for some way to escape, but all he saw was chaos.

The air was filled with dust, the roar of falling stone, and a chorus of unearthly howls and inhuman screams. Fire boiled up from a yawning pit in the center of the cavern, and clouds of bats screeched through the cavern. A crack suddenly split the wall at one side of the cave. Slowly, a slab of stone far larger than a house ripped free, tilted to the side, and toppled to the cave floor. Noah stumbled to his left to avoid a boulder as big as small car, but as he turned around, a lump of limestone the size of a basketball struck him hard in the chest. Something deep inside Noah snapped with a crack. Blinding agony flared, drowning his vision in a red mist of pain. He cried out in agony and fear.

"Noah!"

The vision of the cave shattered like broken glass. Noah blinked and found himself looking up into Kathleen "Harley" Davisidaro's deep chocolate brown eyes. Chestnut hair spilled down to frame her heart-shaped face, and her lips were pressed into a tight line. He saw a smear of dried blood on her forehead and a series of red scratches along her cheek.

"Noah, are you okay?" she asked.

Noah started to laugh, but the sharp pain in his ribs brought his laughter to a rapid stop. "No," he choked out. "I don't think so." Liquid ran across his forehead. Noah brushed it away, and then glanced at his hand. It was damp with a pale pink mixture of sweat and blood.

The vision of the cave was only a dream, but the place and the injuries he had suffered there were very real. Only a few hours ago, Harley and Noah had struggled to escape from the underground headquarters of the clandestine organization known as Umbra. The chaos surrounding their escape had destroyed the caverns and almost cost them their lives.

"What about you?" Noah asked. "Are you all right?"

Harley shrugged. "I'm one big bruise from head to toe, but I don't think I'm really hurt."

The floor under Noah's back jiggled, and he heard a faint rattling sound. He turned his head and looked around him. They were in a small, dimly lit space, surrounded by stacks of folded cloth. Beyond the stacks he could see walls of what looked like corrugated metal. The last thing Noah remembered was stumbling out of the cave after hours of picking their way through darkness. Nothing around him looked the least bit familiar.

"Where are we?" he asked.

"In a truck," Harley replied. She bent down, picked up a dark piece of cloth from the floor, and unfolded it to reveal a T-shirt showing a picture of the Washington Monument. "The driver's on his way to a souvenir stand in D.C.," Harley explained. "He says he'll take us to a hospital."

"Hospital!" Noah sat up in alarm. He coughed and fought back a wave of dizziness. "We can't go to a hospital. Umbra, or Unit 17, or one of the other organizations could be watching for us. If we go to a hospital, we could . . . we could—" He was seized by a coughing fit. Pain lanced through his chest and sparks of light danced in front of his eyes.

Harley knelt down beside him and took his right hand in both of hers. "I know they could be waiting," she said. "But we have to risk it. You're really hurt, Noah. I think you might have broken ribs."

Noah found it difficult to argue when he couldn't even draw a deep breath. He nodded and let his head fall back onto a pillow of stacked T-shirts as Harley released his hand. For a moment, he closed his eyes.

As soon as he did, a new world appeared in front of him. An ancient witch from Umbra had tampered with Noah's mind, freeing a host of paranormal powers that had been planted in him by another of the secret groups called Legion. Behind his closed eyelids, Noah saw a warm, sky blue glow radiating from Harley's body. Further away was another glowing spot—faint lime green—that had to be the driver. The cars passing beside the truck were invisible to his inner vision, but their passengers left behind streaks of yellow and orange and a dozen shades of green.

After a moment, Noah noticed another nearby object visible to this strange inner vision. It was so faint he had missed it at first, but the longer he looked, the brighter this new object became.

Noah opened his eyes, and found Harley still peering down at him. In her hands was a golden orb about the size of a tennis ball. Noah stared at the metallic sphere in surprise. "You still have that thing? I thought it went into the pit."

Harley shook her head. "I found it during the cave-in. I thought it might be worth saving."

"Maybe," Noah admitted.

The golden orb had demonstrated great power. Umbra had used it when they had opened up the new talents in Noah's mind. Later, Noah had hurled the orb at a monstrous thing living in the heart of Umbra's caverns. The orb had driven the creature away, and the resulting explosion had started the cave-in. He had no doubt the orb had power. All the same, Noah found himself wishing it had been buried under tons of black stone.

"Should I keep it?" Harley asked.

Noah started to tell her no, but as he looked up at Harley's face, the word died on his lips.

Besides the dried blood above her eyes, more blood had seeped from some wound hidden under her hair. She had been wearing a woman's business suit when they were captured by Umbra. Now that suit was split open at the seams and torn in a dozen places. The white blouse underneath was also ripped, revealing glimpses of Harley's smooth olive skin—and dark purple bruises. Harley and Noah had both suffered while escaping the caverns, but against all odds, they had both survived. He wondered if the golden orb might have something to do with their miraculous escape.

"Keep it," he said at last. "And you're right. We need to go to a hospital."

Harley smiled in obvious relief. "Good," she said. "After all the work I put into finding you, it would be a real pain if you died on me now."

Noah laughed, then winced. "Don't say anything funny," he begged, raising one hand to his aching chest. "I might be the first person who really *does* die laughing."

"Sorry," Harley replied. "I promise to be dull." She lay the golden sphere gently on the floor of the truck and reached out to Noah. Her fingers brushed lightly over his torn and bloodstained shirt. "Hang on. We should be there in just a couple of minutes."

A thought struck Noah. "What did you tell the truck driver?"

"I said we were in a car accident."

"Didn't he wonder where the car was?" asked Noah.

"I guess we looked bad enough to scare him," Harley replied. "He wanted to call an ambulance, but I was afraid they would start looking around for the car, so I talked him into giving us a ride."

Noah breathed a sign of relief. Harley was probably the most capable person he had ever met. No matter what the problem, she seemed to come up with a solution. "It sounds like you made the right decision," he said. Moving carefully, he eased himself into a sitting position, then gave Harley the best smile he could muster. "Thanks. You saved my life."

Harley shrugged. "You saved mine back there in the cave."

"Yeah, but only after you rescued me from Umbra in the first place."

"But you saved me back by the lake and—"

Noah gave up trying to hold back his laughter. "Okay," he said, chuckling and holding a hand over his aching chest. "We saved each other. Let's hope neither one of us has to do it again."

The truck suddenly swayed, and Noah slid to the side as they went through a sharp turn. Seconds later there was a squeal of brakes, and the vehicle came to a halt.

Noah had a momentary flash of fear. "Are you sure about the truck driver?" he asked.

Harley frowned. "What do you mean?"

"This guy was awfully handy. How do we know he's not another agent?"

"We don't," Harley replied with a shrug. She scooped up the golden orb and held it tightly. "Half the people in Washington seem to be working for one of the secret groups. But it was either go with this guy or wait out there until we both froze to death."

A click from the back of the truck caught Noah's attention, followed by the whine of an electric motor. He blinked against the pale winter sunlight as the rear door began to slide slowly upward.

A figure of a man was silhouetted against the light. He was a big man, with broad shoulders, a thick neck, and arms as wide as smoked hams. In his hand was an odd, jagged shaped object that might be some kind of exotic weapon.

For a moment, Noah thought his fears were confirmed—that the man was an agent who had come to finish the job the falling stones had started. Then the man stepped up into the truck. Noah's image of an muscle-bound killer was replaced by a round-bellied man with pale skin and wind-reddened cheeks. The thick neck was topped with a plump, worried face that was half hidden behind a stiff black beard. The truck driver looked like nothing so much as a young Santa Claus. The strange object in his hand was only a ring of keys.

"Boy, I'm glad to see you sitting up," said the man. He gave a weak grin. "I was afraid you was going to die in my truck."

Noah stretched up his hands, and with Harley's help he struggled to his feet. The effort left him dizzy and fighting back nausea, but he managed to take a step toward the truck driver. "I'm fine," Noah lied. He held out his right hand. "I want to thank you for helping us."

The driver shrugged his vast shoulders. "Nothing to it," he said. "I was heading past this place anyway." He reached out to wrap Noah's hand in a thick-fingered shake.

The moment their fingers touched, Noah let out a gasp of surprise. Umbra's tampering with Noah's mind had left him with more than an ability to see the secret word of psychic energy—he also picked up flashes of things that had happened in the past and things that were going to happen in the future.

The moment that he touched the truck driver's fingers, Noah received a flash that seemed to run all the way through the man's life. The driver's name was

Bill Howe. He lived in Columbus, Ohio, where he had a wife, three kids, and a pair of Labrador retrievers. He had taken the job hauling T-shirts to help out a cousin named Terry.

And he was going to die that afternoon.

As clearly as if he were watching a wide-screen movie, Noah could see the big truck moving down the ramp onto the Reston Parkway. He saw a scrap of metal—part of a discarded muffler—slash through the right front tire, and he saw the truck first skid, then jackknife, then tumble over in the middle of the wide highway. He saw smiling Bill Howe, with his chubby round face, slashed by shattered glass and pinned inside crushed metal.

Noah pulled away from the man and gasped for breath. Touching someone had never produced such a flood of images before. Noah wasn't sure if his new abilities were still growing, or if the driver's fast approaching death had brought on the visions.

"Hey," said the truck driver. "Are you okay?"

"Yeah, sure." Noah stared up at the man's pudgy face and thought of how he'd seen it in the vision—cut and bleeding.

The driver back smiled uncertainly. "I'm glad to hear it. For a second there, you looked like you'd seen a ghost."

"I think maybe I did," Noah said softly. He wasn't sure if the things he saw *had* to come true, or if they just *might* come true. So far, everything he had seen in a vision had happened, but that didn't mean he couldn't try to change things.

"What?" asked the driver.

"Nothing." Noah tightened his grip on the man's hand. "Listen, I want you to promise me you'll stay away from the Reston Parkway today."

"Reston Parkway?" the driver's face clouded with confusion. "How did you know I had a delivery out there?"

"Never mind. Just promise me you'll stay away from there today."

Something in Noah's expression must have convinced the driver that he was serious. The man's smile slipped away and he nodded slowly. "Sure, buddy. Whatever you say."

Noah released the man's hand and sighed in relief. "Good," he said. "That's good." He didn't know if his quick words had really done anything to save the man's life, but at least he had tried.

Harley came forward and put a gentle hand on the driver's meaty arm. While she thanked the man for giving them a ride, Noah climbed slowly to the ground. A moment later, Harley joined Noah in the parking lot. The truck rolled out into the street. Noah only hoped it was safely on its way back to Ohio.

"What was that?" Harley asked, jerking her thumb toward the vanishing truck.

"Nothing," said Noah. "I hope."

The hospital was an older building made from solid yellowish brown stone. It didn't look particularly encouraging, but he saw a large sign reading Emergency over the nearest door.

Noah took a painful breath and followed Harley across the parking lot.

Suddenly, a white-and-red ambulance screamed across the lot, its red and blue lights flashing. It screeched

14

to a halt beside the building. Two paramedics jumped out, ran around to the back, and began to lift out a stretcher. Doctors and nurses appeared from the building wearing loose uniforms of green and blue.

For a moment, Noah thought the scene was just another vision. He walked slowly beside Harley, his chest hurting with every step. Then one of the nurses glanced toward Harley and Noah. Immediately her eyes grew wide. She grabbed a doctor by the arm and pointed across the parking lot.

The doctor sprinted toward them. Her shoulder-length blond hair flew back from her face and the sleeves of her loose surgical scrubs snapped in the cold wind. "What happened to you two?" she shouted as she grew closer.

"A car accident," Harley replied. "We were in a car accident."

The doctor came to a halt an arm's length away. "Well, you certainly look like you were in an accident," she said. Her blue eyes swept over both Noah and Harley. She seemed to immediately pick Noah as the more badly injured of the pair. She reached for the front of Noah's shirt and gently eased open the bloodstained cloth.

Noah shivered as his bare skin was exposed to the cold winter air. He glanced down and saw a dark purple bruise and a crust of dried blood. Just looking at it made him feel queasy. "Is it bad?" he choked out.

The doctor pursed her lips. "We're going to need a chest X ray."

The nurse who had first spotted them jogged up behind the doctor. "What is it?"

"Vehicular accident," the doctor said without looking away from Noah's chest. Her fingers moved over his bruised skin, making Noah cringe. "Go bring out a stretcher and a wheelchair," she instructed the nurse.

"Yes, doctor." The nurse hurried off to follow her instructions.

"I don't need a stretcher," Noah protested. He winced as the doctor's fingers found a particularly tender spot. "I made it this far."

The doctor straightened and looked at Noah with a firm expression. "What's your name?" she asked.

Noah glanced nervously at Harley, but Harley only shrugged. In their effort to get to the hospital, neither of them had planned what to do once they actually made it. If one of the secret groups was still looking for them, just giving a false name wasn't likely to help. "Noah," he said at last. "Noah Templer."

The doctor looked around at Harley. "And you?"

"Kathleen Davisidaro," said Harley.

The doctor looked at them both for a moment, then nodded. "Well, Mr. Templer, Ms. Davisidaro, the next time you have an accident, I suggest you stay with the vehicle. You both may have major internal injuries. Moving around in this condition can cause needless complications."

Noah didn't try to argue. Now that they had actually made it to the hospital, he felt suddenly and incredibly tired. He nodded, then closed his eyes for a moment, watching the pale glow of interns and nurses as they rushed out with the stretcher and wheelchair. He took Harley's hand, gave it a momentary squeeze, then let go as the medical staff helped him onto the stretcher. He felt so exhausted he could barely move his legs.

The ten-second ride across the parking lot was almost enough time for Noah to fall asleep. But the moment he rolled through the doors of the emergency room, he sat bolt upright on the stretcher.

"Lay down," shouted one of the nurses.

Noah barely heard her over the sea of voices bellowing in his mind. The emergency room was full of a million sharp, bitter memories, and each one of them had left behind a ghost. Crowds of ill and injured people clustered all around Noah, their pain so sharp that anguish washed over him like an acid bath. They howled and shrieked their pain—cries that only Noah could hear.

He saw a small boy with blood on his hands and tears rolling down his face. Crowded beside him was a woman with dark bruises circling weary, hopeless eyes. And behind her was a man whose left arm ended in a mangled stump. And behind that a hundred other faces pressed forward. Wounded. Sick. Dying.

Noah looked at the horrible scene and shivered. "I've got to get out of here," he groaned. He grabbed the sides of the stretcher and tried to get down.

The doctor put her hands against Noah's shoulders and pressed him down. "Be still," she commanded. "You'll only hurt yourself if you struggle."

The stretcher was rolled out of the waiting room and down a hallway lined with still more mangled phantoms. Fighting against the pain in his chest, Noah concentrated on separating past, present, and future. Slowly, the bloody visions faded, leaving the hallway empty.

Noah concentrated on keeping the visions away while the doctors X-rayed and examined his wounds. Finally, he was wheeled into a treatment room and put in a bed to wait for the results. Once again, exhaustion began to overcome his pain. He was almost asleep when a touch on his arm shocked him back to wakefulness. Noah shoved away dreams of dark spaces and darker creatures to find Harley standing beside the bed.

"Hi," she said softly.

"Hi." Noah raised his head from the pillow and took a closer look. Harley was wearing a loose gray sweatsuit with a floppy hood spilling over her shoulders and a wide pouch that hung loosely across her slender stomach. Her hair was combed and pulled back from her face in a ponytail. Even with the small bandage on her forehead, she looked a lot more like the beautiful girl he had first met back in Stone Harbor. Seeing her that way made him feel better—it was almost like going home.

"Where'd you get those clothes?" he asked.

"I'm a charity case," Harley replied. "They've got a box of stuff they hand out to homeless people. Since my clothes were torn to ribbons, they let me browse." She plucked at the oversized sweatshirt and frowned. "Not exactly the height of fashion, but I guess I can't complain."

Noah smiled. "On you, it looks good." He expected Harley to be pleased at the compliment, but the frown stayed on her face. "What's wrong?" he asked.

Harley pursed her lips and looked around the room

for a moment, then leaned in close to Noah's bed. "Did you tell anyone my nickname was Harley?" she whispered.

"No. Why?"

"When I went past the admissions desk, someone asked me if that was my name."

Noah sat up in alarm, his ribs protesting sharply. "You think Umbra's been here?"

Harley shrugged. "I don't know." She pulled out a folded piece of yellow paper and handed it across to Noah. "Someone called and left this message."

Noah took the paper and scanned it. The handwriting was hurried, and whoever had taken the note had put down only the bare minimum of words.

Harley Davisidaro
Spotted you checking in. We're at the office.
Come immediately. Scott.

"Scott?" Noah asked, looking up. The name sounded familiar.

"One of the two guys who Dee and I met up here is named Scott," she explained. "Scott and Kenyon were there when we found you at that abandoned store. Remember?"

"No." Noah shook his head slowly. "I was really out of it." Noah vaguely remembered that he had seen Dee Janes. Dee was an old friend of his from Stone Harbor, though Noah had no idea how she had ended up in Washington. He could remember little about the two guys who had helped Harley and Dee. "You think this note really came from Scott? How could he have spotted us?"

She shrugged. "I don't know. Scott's pretty good with computers. Maybe he picked up our names when they went into the hospital's database."

Noah passed the bit of yellow paper back to Harley. "Is there any way for you to call them back?"

Harley shook her head. "Not that I can think of," she said. She bit her lip again. "I guess they're over at the office building where they had their things before. I'm really worried about Dee. That office building is the place where Umbra found us. They could always come back and get the others."

The door to the examining room swung open and the woman doctor with blond hair stepped in with a clipboard in her hands. She gave Harley a critical look. "Are you supposed to be up, Ms. Davisidaro?"

"The nurse said I could come to check on Noah," Harley replied.

The doctor seemed skeptical of this information, but she let it go. "I'm Doctor Burris," she said, directing her words to Noah. "I've had a chance to look over your X rays, and I think I have good news." She pulled a sheet of darkened film from the clipboard and held it out where Noah could see.

Noah squinted at the sheet. He could see the light arcs of his ribs and the bones of his shoulders. He didn't see anything that was obviously wrong. "What am I supposed to be looking for?" he asked.

Dr. Burris raised a slim finger and tapped the center of the X-ray. "Three of your ribs are cracked."

"And that's supposed to be good news?" asked Noah.

"Relatively," replied the doctor. She put the X-ray plate back in the folder and looked at Noah. "Your ribs have only hairline fractures. They should heal on their own in a few weeks. Compare that to surgery, a punctured lung, or a body cast, and I think you'll agree that you got off lucky."

Noah had to nod. "I guess it could have been worse."

"A lot worse," Dr. Burris agreed.

"So are you going to let him leave now?" Harley asked.

The doctor shook her head. "Not just yet. We've got a few more tests to run. We should have you out of here in a couple of hours—though we may want to admit you overnight for observation." With that, the doctor turned and left the room.

"A couple of hours," Harley repeated. Her forehead creased in frustration.

Noah thought for a moment. "How far is it to the office Scott mentioned in the message?"

"Not far," Harley answered. "I asked the receptionist. It's only a couple of miles away."

Noah reached out and took Harley's hand. "Why don't you go over there and check on them while I finish up here?"

The worry lines on Harley's forehead grew deeper. "Are you sure?" she asked. "We've been apart so long. . . . I hate to leave you again."

The truth was that Noah felt the same way. He had only known Harley for a matter of weeks, and for a good part of that time he had been held prisoner by Umbra, but there was no one he felt closer to on earth. He wanted Harley to stay. More than that, he was *scared* to be without her.

"I'll be fine," he said with a confidence he didn't

feel. He worked hard to come up with a reassuring smile. "Go on. You can all come back here and pick me up together."

Harley gave his hand a quick squeeze and returned his smile. "You stay right here," she said. "If you go anywhere, I'm going to be mad." She reached into the pouch of her sweatshirt and pulled out the golden orb. "What about this thing?" she asked. "Should I leave it with you?"

Noah shook his head quickly. He didn't know if holding onto the orb was a good idea, but he was sure he didn't want it. "You keep it."

"All right." Harley shoved the little metal ball back into her sweatshirt. "You're going to wait here, right?"

"Absolutely," replied Noah.

Harley bent down quickly and planted a brief kiss on Noah's lips. Then, before he could say another word, she hurried out of the room.

Noah fell back onto the bed. The kiss had surprised him. As far as he could remember, he and Harley had never kissed before. They had barely known each other before they began their private war with the secret organizations. They had been joined together by their struggle—partners in survival. Somewhere along the line, things had changed. He wasn't sure just how he felt about Harley, but she was far more than just a friend.

Maybe, he thought, when all this weird stuff is over. . . . He stopped and shook his head. First they had to get Harley's father back from the paramilitary group named Unit 17 and discover the truth about Noah and his own relationship to the group called Legion. Things were a long way from over.

They were a long way from being through with the weird stuff.

Noah turned and looked through the open door. She'll only be gone for half an hour, he told himself. Maybe forty-five minutes. He felt more than a little ridiculous for being so worried, but he couldn't help it—things always seemed to go better when they were together.

The door of the room opened again, and Dr. Burris returned. "We're going to take you back down to imaging," she announced. "There's a problem in your X rays."

"Problem?" Noah raised up on one elbow and looked at the doctor. "I thought you said my X rays were good news."

"Good news about your ribs." Dr. Burris took out the dark film sheet again. "It's this spot in your shoulder I'm worried about."

On the film, Noah saw a fuzzy white patch floating above the bones of his left shoulder. A cold sensation came over him.

Back in Stone Harbor, a man named Cain had told Noah that there was a device planted under the skin of his shoulder—a device that sent information to the group called Legion. According to Cain, the device had been disabled, but Noah wasn't sure if he could trust Cain. The man had lied about being an FBI agent, but he had also helped Noah and Harley get out of some tough situations. Noah had been so worried about the hidden device that he had gone to his doctor in Stone Harbor and had an X ray made. That X ray had shown nothing. But the plate that

Dr. Burris held certainly showed *something* hiding in the flesh of his shoulder.

Noah reached out to touch the fuzzy spot on the X ray. "What is that?"

"We're not sure," replied Dr. Burris. "Possibly a piece of debris forced under your skin during the accident. Once we get an MRI, we'll have a better idea of what we're looking at."

The door to the examining room flew open and a nurse leaned in. "Dr. Burris, we need you in trauma one right away."

Dr. Burris glanced at the nurse and nodded. "I'm coming," she said. Then she turned back to Noah. "I'll send someone to collect you in just a moment." Without waiting for a reply, the doctor put Noah's folder down on the foot of the bed and left the room in a run.

Noah picked up the X-ray plate and stared at the tiny spot of white. The image wasn't clear, but he thought he could make outlines of something blocky, and somehow bristly, hiding in the center of that glowing patch.

The door to the room swung open again. Noah looked up, expecting to see a nurse or intern. Instead, he saw a tall, thin man dressed in the blue scrubs and white coat of a Doctor. The man had deeply tanned skin and hair that was an odd shade of blond— yellow as a ripe banana.

"Are you Noah?" asked the man.

Noah started to nod then caught himself. Something was wrong. Ever since he entered the hospital, he had been pushing away his abilities. It kept the flood of horrifying images away, but it also kept

Noah from seeing anything about this strange man. "Who are you?"

"A friend," said the man. He held up something the size and shape of a television remote control. Tiny green-and-red lights sparkled across the instrument as the man's spidery fingers tapped on a series of buttons. "A very close friend."

A wave of panic rushed over Noah, washing away the pain in his chest. He hurled the barriers away from his mind and saw a cold white light hovering around the strange man's body. Noah rolled off the side of the bed, grabbed the metal base of an IV stand, and came up holding the pole like a baseball bat. "Stay back," he warned.

"Come now, Noah," the man said in a mocking voice. The halo of light around him flickered and pulsed in time with his words. "That's no way to act." His fingers danced again over his hand held device.

Immediately, Noah felt a sharp tingling in his shoulder that spread over the rest of his body. The IV stand slipped from his numb fingers and crashed to the floor. His knees wobbled, then gave way. Noah crumpled to the floor. He tried to get back up, but his hands and feet only flopped like jellyfish on the tiles. He tried to shout for the Doctors and nurses that were just outside the room, but all that came out was a weak whisper.

The man with the yellow hair knelt down beside Noah. "Just relax," he said. "Don't fight, and we'll have you out of here in a few minutes."

"You're from Legion," Noah choked out.

"Yes," the man said. "And so are you."

X TWO

Harley shivered as she walked down the street. The clothes provided by the hospital were better than the tattered rags she had been wearing, but they weren't nearly warm enough to hold up to a bitter Washington, D. C. winter.

She wished she could take a cab, or even the metro. But what little money she had was back at the office building where Scott and Kenyon had made their headquarters—that is, her money was there unless someone had taken it. Noah and Harley had been removed from the building by a group of FBI agents and by the treacherous Umbra agent, Billie, who was masquerading as an FBI official. If the FBI had searched the building, Harley's tiny roll of cash was probably locked up in some evidence room along with all of Scott and Kenyon's computer gear.

She reached a corner and paused as the tall structure of Water Tower Place came into view. The office building had been under construction by a company owned by Kenyon's parents. But when his parents had crossed Unit 17, they had been killed in a mysterious "accident." Construction had come to a halt. The tall office building stood empty and unfinished.

Harley didn't see any cars in the parking lot, and she didn't notice anyone hanging around—which didn't mean a whole army of agents couldn't be hiding right around the corner.

Finally, the cold and her own impatience got her moving again. Harley walked briskly along the sidewalk with her eyes fixed on an empty billboard some blocks away. She hoped that anyone seeing her would think she was just passing by. At the last second, she darted to the side and grabbed the handle of the building's front door. To Harley's surprise, it was open. She stepped in quickly and pulled it closed behind her.

The lobby of Water Tower Place was just as she remembered it: unpainted walls of bare plasterboard, supplies stacked in corners, and the elevator doors gaping open. Though she saw nothing unusual in the lobby, Harley felt a sudden sharp increase in tension as she crossed the tiled floor and entered the middle elevator.

She punched the button for the twelfth floor and leaned back against the rear wall of the elevator. Harley didn't know what to expect. She could find Dee, and Kenyon, and Scott all safe and waiting for her. Or the door might open to reveal an army of the terrible dark men—creatures of shadow and bitter cold under the control of Umbra. Harley's breath came in shallow pants and her heart pounded in her chest as the elevator began to rise. A soft bell sounded her arrival at the twelfth floor. Harley braced herself for what she might see as the brushed metal doors of the elevator began to open.

As soon as the door slid open, she could tell the place was deserted. The twelfth floor was one big unfinished space, with a bare concrete floor and electrical conduits running overhead. There were no walls, and even the elevator shafts lacked doors. Except for the elevator that Harley had ridden up in, they remained open on dangling cables and there was a long dark fall to the lobby.

No one came up to greet Harley, and nothing rushed to attack her. She stepped out of the elevator and let the doors close behind her. "Hello," she called without any real hope of an answer. "Dee? Scott?" The only reply was a faint echo.

Walking slowly around the corner away from the elevators, Harley saw the place where Kenyon and Scott had made their headquarters. It had been a small but neat space, full of supplies and computers—an island of order. That island was gone.

Sleeping cots lay broken and turned on their sides. Storage boxes had been overturned, their contents sprayed across the floor. Clothing lay scattered along with loose papers and the contents of the trash cans. The tables where a pair of sophisticated computers had sat were empty. Harley could find no sign that Scott, Kenyon, or Dee had been back since the raid.

She let out a long shuddering breath. The tension she had felt since entering the building eased, only to be replaced by sadness. "Dee," she said again, not expecting an answer.

Harley felt it was her fault that Dee had come to Washington in the first place. The others, Scott and Kenyon, had their own reasons to pursue the secret societies. But Dee had only been trying to help find Noah and Harley's missing father. Now it was Dee who was missing, and Harley had no idea where to look for her.

She walked through the scattered remains of the headquarters, kicking away loose clothing and papers. She spotted a pair of shoes so small they had to belong to Dee, and stepped over a jacket so obviously expensive that it had to be Kenyon's.

Harley noticed a photograph peeking out of Kenyon's jacket pocket. She picked it up and peered at it. It was a picture of Kenyon, staring seriously out at the camera. In the shot, he was flanked by two middle-aged people, obviously his mother and father. Surpringly, a small boy of about eight years old stood in front of Kenyon. If Kenyon had a little brother, he sure hadn't mentioned him to Harley. She felt a pang of sadness and anger as she looked at Kenyon's parents. They had been senselessly killed by Unit 17.

She tucked the picture into the back pocket of her pants for safekeeping and continued to search the area.

A spot of shiny black among the mess on the floor caught Harley's eye. She bent down excitedly as she saw that it was her cheap vinyl backpack. She was even more pleased to find a couple of shirts, a single pair of jeans, and a small roll of bills still nestled inside. In fact, almost everything that Harley owned was safely in the bag. Only one item was missing—the small leather-bound journal recording her father's work.

She dropped to her hands and knees and pawed frantically among the heap of debris. Since his disappearance, the journal was the one thing that Harley still had from her father. It was her one clue to what had happened to him—and to his secret past.

Harley's father had always told her that he worked on new radar systems for the military. But the experiments recorded in the book mentioned nothing about detecting enemy planes and missiles. Instead, the journal recorded experiments on paranormal abilities. Harley hadn't understood much of what was written in the book, but she had figured out enough to know that it was important. The journal might lead her to her father—or to the truth about a mother she had thought was long dead.

"Where is it?" Harley mumbled as she pushed away tattered papers and a sack from a hamburger place. "It has to be here."

From across the empty room, Harley heard the solid click of a door latch opening.

She froze. She turned her head slowly and stared through the gloom. Harley heard the sound again as the door clicked closed. Someone was coming. She could see a dim shape moving in the shadows. Footsteps echoed from the bare walls.

Harley scanned the space around her for a weapon. She found the broken leg of a folding chair and snatched it from the floor. The little metal tube was so light that it was all but useless. Harley hoped she would *look* dangerous at least.

Slowly, she rose to her feet. "Who's there?" she asked, trying to keep her voice steady and calm.

The figure stepped into the light. It was a middle-aged man with a thick barrel chest and thinning hair. He wore an immaculate dark blue suit with a red kerchief in the breast pocket. A gray mustache bristled above his thin lips. His posture was as stiff as a soldier in a parade. "Good afternoon, Ms. Davisidaro."

Without thinking, Harley took a step backward, away from the man. "Braddock," she whispered.

"Yes," the man agreed. He approached her, closing the distance between them to no more than ten feet.

His iron gray eyes glistened in the pale light. "I'm certainly pleased we got this chance to meet again."

Harley raised her pitiful club and shook her head. "I'm not," she said. "The last time we met, you tortured me."

Braddock shrugged. "A highly regrettable incident."

"I'm sure," Harley said sarcastically.

Braddock had been the commander of the Unit 17 base near Stone Harbor. When Harley's father had disappeared while working on that base, Braddock had tried to keep Harley under his control. But she had escaped from Braddock. With Noah's help, she had penetrated the secret heart of the base and witnessed its destruction. At the time, Harley had thought Braddock was dead. But she had encountered the man again at a strange medical facility in New Jersey. Harley had seen a woman in that facility—a woman in a glass tube filled with some awful yellow fluid—a woman who just might be Harley's real mother. Braddock had captured Harley there and tortured her in ways she didn't even want to think about. If it wasn't for the man called Cain, Harley felt sure she would have died in that place.

"What do you want?" she snarled at Braddock.

The commander gave a thin smile. "It's not just what I want," he said. "It's what you want." He reached inside his jacket.

Harley jumped back. "What are you doing?"

Braddock laughed. "Don't worry. I'm not pulling a weapon." His hand emerged from his coat holding a familiar small book. "I believe you were looking for this."

"That's mine!" Harley took a quick step toward

him and reached out her free hand for the journal.

The commander pulled the book away. "Is it?"

Harley gritted her teeth. "Yes. Give it to me."

"Perhaps." Braddock flipped open the cover of the book and thumbed through the first few pages. "I don't think this book is yours," he said coolly. "I believe this actually belongs to one of my researchers. This book records highly classified information regarding experiments which we have worked decades to perfect. I'm not sure it should rest in the hands of a child."

Harley weighed the metal rod in her hand. It was light, but she figured it would still deliver a nasty whack to Braddock's face if she swung it hard enough. "Give me the book," she demanded.

"I'll be happy to," Braddock replied. "If you'll give me what I want."

The offer made Harley pause. In the past, Braddock had tried to kill her or to hurt her. He had never tried to bargain with her. She didn't trust Braddock, but listening to him might give her some clues to what was really going on.

"What do you want?" she asked.

"Nothing that you yourself don't want," the commander replied with another thin smile. "I want to find your father."

"What?" Harley blinked in surprise. "But . . . but you're the one that took my father away!"

Braddock shook his head. "No. We've never had him."

Anger tightened Harley's jaw. "I'm not grotesquely stupid," she said. "My father disappeared on your base. You told me that he was on assignment."

"Another highly unfortunate event," replied the

commander. "Believe me, it was as much of a loss to us as it was to you. However, I'm now prepared to tell you the truth regarding this incident."

Harley almost laughed. "I don't think you *can* tell the truth. Where is my father?"

Braddock gave an elaborate sigh. "I'm afraid that's a little difficult to explain."

"Try me."

"All right." The Unit 17 commander turned and began to pace across the floor. "Your father had worked for me for over ten years. He was a brilliant man. You should be proud."

Harley started to reply, then stopped and pressed her lips together. She had always been proud of her father, but she didn't want to believe Braddock. The father she remembered was kind and funny, but always a little sad too. Harley didn't want to believe that her father could have had anything to do with Braddock.

"Your father investigated many interesting fields," the commander continued, "but for the last few years, his energies were concentrated in one area. He was attempting to develop . . ." Braddock trailed off and waved a hand through the air as if searching for the right word. "A new form of transportation," he added at last.

"Transportation?" Harley shook her head. She had expected something strange, but Braddock's words didn't seem to make any sense. "Like a train or car?"

"Something far more marvelous," Braddock replied, his eyes shining. "The problem is, he seems to have become stuck in transit. We need your help to get him out."

Harley shook her head slowly. "I don't know what you're talking about," she said.

Braddock opened his mouth to reply, but at that moment a soft beep sounded from inside his jacket. He reached in again and came out with a tiny cellular phone. "Excuse me," he said to Harley. Then he flipped the phone open. "Yes?"

From the corner of the room, Harley thought she heard another sound. She peered into the shadows and saw nothing, but after a moment the sound came again. "What's going on?" she asked.

With a flip of his wrist, Braddock closed the phone and returned it to his pocket. "Nothing," he said. He smiled again. This time it was a real smile—the smile of someone very pleased with the world.

Seeing that smile gave Harley goosebumps. If Braddock was happy, then she was in trouble. She backed slowly away from Unit 17 commander. "You were telling me about my father," she said. At the same time, she shifted her eyes left and right, looking for any route of escape.

"Yes, I was." Braddock ran a finger over his mustache. "However, there's no need for that now. All exits to this building have been secured, and our scans show that you have what we need." He held out his hand. "The time for talk is over. Give me the device."

Harley shook her head. "I don't know what you're talking about."

The smile vanished instantly from Braddock's face. "Do you think I'm *stupid?*" he snarled. "You're carrying a device that amplifies the entire Trans-alpha range. Give it to me now, or I will take it from you by whatever means necessary."

"I don't—," Harley started, then she stopped in midsentence. The golden orb. That had to be the device that Braddock was after.

Harley resisted an urge to reach into the pouch of her sweatshirt and see if the sphere was still there. She looked straight into Braddock's eyes and shook her head. "I'm not giving you anything until you bring back my father."

The commander gave an ugly laugh. "That's just what I'm going to do." He turned and looked into the corner of the room. "Get her!" he called.

A pair of men in dark blue uniforms burst out of the shadows. They ran toward Harley with their hands outstretched and expressions of grim determination on their hard faces.

Harley hurled the metal pipe at Braddock. As the Unit 17 leader ducked, Harley jumped past him and sprinted for the elevators.

From behind her Harley heard a sound like a vacuum cleaner, or maybe a power saw. As the concrete floor at her feet chipped and shattered, throwing up a cloud of dust, Harley realized someone was shooting at her.

"*Cease fire*, you idiot!" ordered Braddock. "We need the girl alive."

Harley felt glad to hear that. She was a fast runner, but not faster than a bullet. She turned the corner and charged toward the single functioning elevator. Close behind her came the sound of boot heels racketing on the hard floor.

She slammed her palm against the button, and at once

the elevator chimed. But as the door opened, another blue-suited soldier emerged. Harley spun around and saw another two close behind her. She felt a scream building down inside her as she realized that she was trapped.

The soldiers slowed to a stop a few feet away. "Get down on your knees," one of the men said. His voice was as flat and as emotionless as a robot's. "Put your hands behind your head and stay where you are."

Gritting her teeth, Harley started to obey. Then she spotted something in the shadow of the open elevator shaft just to her right. With one last glance toward the soldiers, she slung her backpack over her shoulder and jumped into the darkness.

Her fingers caught the rungs of a metal ladder built into the shaft. The ladder trembled with the impact, and Harley's grip came loose. For a stomach-churning moment she was falling toward the unseen ground more than a hundred feet below. Then she caught the ladder again and began to climb down as fast as she could.

"Give up, Ms. Davisidaro!" came Braddock's voice from over her head. "Even if you climb all the way to the ground, my men are waiting."

Harley ignored him. She would worry about the men on the ground once she was *on* the ground. The ladder shook again. Harley looked up and saw the boots of a soldier ten feet above her head.

She climbed on. The ladder continued to shake as the soldier descended toward her. Harley's breath came hard as she pumped arms and legs, arms and legs, going down so fast she risked a fall at any moment. The tenth floor went past, and the ninth.

When Harley dared look up again, the soldier was

closer. Only three feet separated her head and the hard soles of his black books. She cursed in frustration. Her arms and legs were beginning to tremble from the strain and effort. She was going as fast as she could, but it wasn't fast enough.

As the opening for the eighth floor appeared, Harley dived out of the elevator shaft and ran for the stairway at the corner of the building. She went no more than ten feet before she tripped and fell over a stack of supplies. Unlike the empty twelfth floor, the eighth had been partly finished when construction came to a halt. The bare metal framework of walls divided the space. Sheets of plasterboard were heaped in stacks, turning the floor into a dimly lit maze.

The soldier in the elevator shaft jumped out. "Surrender," he said. "I will use force."

The flatness of the man's voice only made his threats more frightening. Harley got to her feet and scrambled away, dodging between the stacks of hardware.

From somewhere behind her there was a loud crash, then a muttered curse. Harley was pleased to hear it. The Unit 17 soldier might climb fast and talk scary, but he wasn't superhuman.

While the soldier was still thrashing his way through a stack of aluminum beams, Harley ducked behind a heap of paneling. Her arms and legs ached. It was not only the climbing down the ladder that had worn her out, it was days without sleep, a hundred small injuries, and hours of walking through dark caverns. Harley was in no shape to run a race with Braddock's agents.

Just as she was thinking about the Unit 17

commander, the door in the corner opened. Braddock marched in with two soldiers close behind. "Greerson! Are you in here?" he shouted.

"Yes, sir!" called the soldier who had followed Harley down the elevator shaft. "Our target is here."

"Spread out," Braddock ordered his men. "Be methodical. If she's here we'll find her."

Harley crouched low and tried to quiet her ragged breathing. Once again, she felt the net closing around her. She ground her teeth in frustration.

"The north end is clean!" shouted one of the soldiers.

"Divide the remainder," Braddock replied. "Someone get a scanner down here. The device she's carrying will give her away."

A soldier passed within a dozen feet of Harley's hiding place. She ducked down quickly, then slowly raised her head again. She saw something different on the far wall—something that might be her only chance.

One of the windows of the building had been removed. In its place was the mouth of a huge yellow plastic pipe. Broken bits of lumber and twisted metal were stacked near the pipe, ready to be tossed out.

Harley looked at the open mouth of the pipe for the space of two heartbeats. Either it was going to lead her to safety, or to death. After what she had experienced, there was no way she was going to let herself be captured by Unit 17.

Harley rose to her feet.

"There!" shouted a soldier. "She's over there."

A scream came boiling from Harley's mouth. It wasn't a cry of fear, it was a shout of anger and frustration and defiance. It started in her stomach, gained force in her chest, and roared through her throat in a raw banshee wail.

Still screaming, Harley ran across the room and dived headfirst into the pipe.

Shooting down the pipe was like being inside the steepest water slide on earth, only without the water. The yellow interior of the pipe went by at a maddening blur as Harley slid at a speed just short of falling. Friction burned her hands. She pulled up her arms and strained to keep her face from striking the plastic.

The pipe leveled out slightly toward the end, and Harley was just starting to hope for a gentle landing when she emerged like a torpedo from the end of the pipe. For a moment she was airborne, arcing above the blacktop parking lot. Then she crashed into a metal Dumpster amid a jumble of broken plasterboard.

To her own great surprise, she lived.

Harley stood up, coughed, and waved away a cloud of plaster dust. Her backpack had come lose during the trip down the pipe, but it was lying not far away. She retrieved it, climbed over the side of the Dumpster, then looked up toward the dark windows of Water Tower Place. There was no sign of Braddock and his men, but Harley had no doubt they were watching her.

She reached in the pouch of her oversized sweatshirt and closed her fingers on something hard and metallic. Miraculously, after all she had done, the golden orb was still in place.

Harley pulled out the metal ball and held it over her head. "It's mine!" she shouted at the silent building. "It's mine, and you're never going to get it!"

Noah Templer woke up.

The strangest thing was that he couldn't remember going to sleep. He remembered the fight with Umbra, the dark hours spent walking through the cave, and pain. Then nothing.

It was hard to remember. It was even hard to think. Every time Noah tried to get hold of a memory, it broke apart and drifted away, leaving only disconnected images behind. He felt as though his mind had been packed in cold grease—too slick to let a thought in, too thick to let a memory out.

Noah tried to sit up and look around, but his arms wouldn't move. Neither would his legs. One part of his mind insisted that he should be worried by this paralysis. More than worried—panicked. But Noah felt nothing. His emotions seemed almost as frozen as his body.

With a supreme effort, Noah turned his head slowly to one side. He saw walls painted a soft pastel blue and a window with blinds that let in bars of yellow sunshine. There was a painting of flowers on the wall and a single chair in the corner. Close beside the bed, he could see a simple shelf that held a small machine. Glowing red numbers flashed on the front of the machine in time with a soft beep. Just to the right of the machine, Noah saw a silvery metal pole holding two bags of some clear fluid. Tubes led off the bottom of the bags. Moving his eyes, Noah could trace the path of the tubes down to his right arm.

Hospital. The word came to him from far away. He was in a hospital.

For long minutes, he lay still, processing that single word. If he was in a hospital, then how did he get here? His sluggish mind pulled up a memory of tonsils when he was a kid, but that was years back. There had been a pain in his chest, he remembered that much. That had to be the reason he was here.

A woman dressed in pale pink came into the room and walked directly over to the machine on the shelf. She pulled out a clipboard and scribbled something, then checked the contents of the clear bags. She never even looked at Noah. The woman turned and was about to leave.

"Wait," said Noah. At least, that's what he tried to say. His voice didn't seem any more cooperative than his limbs, and something seemed to be blocking his throat. All that came from his mouth was a very weak moan.

Even so, it was enough to get the woman's attention. She looked around at Noah. Immediately her eyes went wide. "You're awake," she said. The idea seemed to surprise her.

Noah managed to nod slightly.

"Hang on," said the woman. "I'll be right back." She left the room at a trot.

Within seconds, she returned. This time she brought a man in a loose white jacket and hair that was butter yellow. "See, Doctor," said the woman. "He's awake."

"Well," the man replied slowly. "His eyes are open. But is he responsive?"

"He nodded. And I think he tried to talk."

"Did he?" The Doctor leaned over Noah. "Is this true, Noah? Are you ready to talk to us?"

Noah nodded again. The Doctor looked familiar. Noah tried to remember where he had seen the man, but the harder he tried, the weaker his memory seemed.

The Doctor smiled. "It appears you really are awake," he said. "Hang on a moment." The Doctor looked over at the woman. "Go notify the family. I'm sure they'll want to know right away."

The woman—the nurse, Noah remembered the word, the nurse—left the room while the Doctor pulled a chair close to the bed. "Now, Noah," the Doctor began, "I'm Doctor Ripley. I'm going to remove the NG feeding tube so you can talk. This will be a little unpleasant, but it won't take long."

The Doctor's hands reached down to Noah's face and fiddled with something around his nose. Tape came loose with a soft ripping sound and Noah felt a sting on his cheeks. Then the Doctor began to tug and that tiny sting was forgotten. Removing the tube was more than unpleasant—it was horrible. Noah could feel movement all the way from his nose down to his throat. He wanted to cough, or choke, but the slithering tube was in his way. As it pulled loose from his throat, it left a trail of fire behind. By the time the tip of the feeding tube came loose, Noah felt as if he had been cleaned out by a red-hot wire.

"There," said the Doctor, setting the NG tube aside. "That should make talking a lot easier. Can you tell me your name?"

"N . . . ," Noah choked out, bringing fresh pain from his raw throat. "Nnn . . . ah."

The Doctor put a hand on his shoulder. "Very good," he said. "It'll take you just a little practice, but in a short while you'll be talking up a storm. Now, do you know where you are?"

Noah s hook his head. "Hospital?"

"Yes," the Doctor agreed with a nod. "You're in the hospital at Westerberg. Do you know where that is?"

It took a moment for Noah to remember Westerberg. It was a town along the coast highway, bigger than Stone Harbor, but not big enough to really be called a city. "Yes," he said. "I know."

"That's wonderful," said the Doctor. "Now, if you can hold on for a few minutes, I'll send a nurse in to look over you. We need to run a few tests. Okay?"

Noah nodded slowly. Tests. The word brought a flash of memory. He remembered now. He had been in a hospital. He and Harley had gone there to get treatment after escaping from Umbra's underground headquarters. But that hospital had been in Washington D.C., not Westerberg. He couldn't begin to think of how he had moved over five hundred miles.

Before Noah could think of a question, the Doctor left the room. For a few minutes, Noah had nothing to look at but the blue walls and the slowly moving bars of sunshine on the floor. Finally another nurse appeared.

"Well, isn't it nice to see you awake?" she said. "You've had a long sleep."

"Long sleep," repeated Noah. "How long?"

The nurse looked a little worried. "Didn't Doctor Ripley explain this to you?"

"No. What happened?"

The woman reached out and patted Noah's motionless hand. "I'm not sure how much I should say. You were in a car accident, and you've been unconscious. I think I should wait for the Doctor before giving any more details." She leaned back in her chair and gave Noah a sympathetic smile. "Don't worry. I'm sure Doctor Ripley will explain everything."

Noah tried to remember anything about a car wreck, but he could recall nothing. He had been hurt in a cave-in, not a car wreck. Then he remembered—Harley had told the Doctor that the two of them had been in an accident. That had to be the answer.

He laid his head back on the pillow and closed his eyes. If the Doctors had believed Harley's story, that explained why they thought he was in car wreck, but it sure didn't explain how he had gotten to Westerberg. He started to say something else to the nurse, then he stopped and frowned. Something was missing.

It took a moment for Noah to realize what was wrong—the glow. Ever since Umbra had broken the barriers in his mind, Noah had been able to close his eyes and see a glow from the body of every human being. But he saw no glow from the nurse. He turned his head slowly, pointing his face toward the door leading to the rest of the hospital. He saw nothing. Even from his own body, which had seemed bright before, there was no sign of light.

Noah took a deep breath and tried his best to concentrate. He searched the darkness behind his eyelids for some sign of the glowing thread that led from his body up to the tangled mass known as the nexus. He found nothing. The nexus itself, which had always been there like a great glowing cloud hanging over everything, was gone.

"Did he lose consciousness again?" he heard the doctor ask.

Noah opened his eyes and saw that Dr. Ripley was back in the room along with another man dressed in green scrubs. "No, I'm awake."

Ripley smiled. "Very good. Come on, let's get you sitting up." The Doctor slid his hands under Noah's left arm, and the man in green took the right. Together they raised him into a sitting position.

"How do you feel, Noah?" asked the doctor.

"Sleepy," Noah replied.

Dr. Ripley chuckled. "I would have thought you'd had enough of that. Let me see you do a little work. Can you move your legs for me, Noah?"

Noah tried, but his legs remained stubbornly still. A sharp edge of fear entered his mind. Noah's legs might still be frozen, but his emotions were thawing quickly. "What happened?" he asked. "Am I paralyzed?"

"We don't know that," said Dr. Ripley. "What about your hands, Noah, can you move them?"

"I'll try." Noah strained for all he was worth. He had been a track star and a basketball star. He poured all the effort of a hundred meter dash into making his right hand move. Slowly, his thumb and first finger came together. Noah felt a wave of both disappointment and relief.

"That's wonderful," said Dr. Ripley.

Noah frowned. "Why am I like this?" he asked. "What happened?"

Dr. Ripley looked around at the nurse and the man in green. "I need a moment alone with this patient."

"Of course, Doctor." The others in the room left quickly.

Dr. Ripley grabbed the chair, pulled it close to the bed, and sat down. "Noah, what's the last thing you remember?"

Noah wasn't sure what he should say. The last thing he remembered was Harley talking to him in the hospital in Washington—she had kissed him. But he wasn't sure he should mention Harley or where they had been together. "I don't know," he said at last. "I think I was out of town."

Dr. Ripley nodded. "Yes, you were on your way to Lake Malone. Does that ring a bell?"

"Lake Malone?" Noah knew the place well enough, but his last memories were from near Washington, D.C., hundreds of miles from both Stone Harbor and Lake Malone. "I don't remember being there."

"That's not unusual in cases of this kind. Memory can be disturbed by such accidents."

"I don't remember any accident," said Noah.

"No, you probably don't," the Doctor told him gently. "Memories from immediately before the accident are generally the last to return." The Doctor pulled a small notebook from the pocket of his white jacket and flipped through the pages. "Do you have any idea how long you've been here?"

Noah shook his head. "The nurse said it had been a long time."

The Doctor's head came up quickly and she frowned. "Did she? I'll have to talk to her about that."

"How long?" Noah asked. "How long have I been here?"

Dr. Ripley drew a deep breath. "Almost two months, Noah."

If he hadn't already been lying down, Noah thought he would have fallen in shock. Two months. If he had been flat on his back in a hospital for so long, anything could have happened. And there was no telling how long he and Harley had been back in Stone Harbor before the wreck. If Noah had forgotten going home, he might have forgotten almost anything. "Do you know what happened to my friend?" he asked.

The Doctor looked down at his notebook. "According to my notes, you were alone in the car when the accident occurred." There was a knock at the door. The Doctor looked up from his notes and smiled. "Ah, here comes someone who can tell you all about it."

Noah turned his head slightly and was amazed at what he saw. "Mom?"

His mother ran to the side of the bed and grabbed Noah's hand. Tears stood out in her blue eyes and her forehead was creased with worry. "Oh, honey. You don't know how much we've waited for this day." She stopped and sniffed back tears. "We were afraid you'd never . . . never . . . ," Her voice trailed away into sobs.

"It's all right, Mom," Noah said. With an effort, he gripped his mother's hand. "I'm awake."

Noah noticed movement in the corner of his vision. A moment later, his father stepped into view. "Son," he said in a softer voice than Noah had ever heard him use. Noah was shocked to see that there were tears in his father's eyes. William Templer had made millions in real estate, but he was still an old bay fisherman at heart. Noah had seen his father boil in rage and seen him go cold as ice. But he had never before seen him cry.

His father wiped his tears away with the back of his big hand. "Well, son, you've had a lot of people pulling for you. Did the Doctor tell you about it?"

Noah shook his head. "No."

"This room has had visitors almost around the clock. Almost every member of the basketball team has sat with you, and some of the track team too. Even the coach stayed with you one night."

It was nice information, but it wasn't what Noah wanted to hear. "What about Harley?" he asked. "Is she okay?"

His father frowned and shook his head. "I'm afraid I don't know anyone named Harley. Is that another student from school?"

Noah tried to remember if he had ever told his parents about Harley. He was almost sure he had. The confusion and excitement he had felt at seeing his parents was suddenly laced with suspicion. He had already seen how some of the people in Umbra and the other groups could change their appearance. These people might not be his parents at all. And even if they were, Noah had another reason to be cautious.

"She's a girl on the track team," he said carefully.

"I'll talk to the coach tomorrow," said his father. He smiled broadly and put his hand on Noah's shoulder. "You don't know how good it is to talk to you."

With a final sniff, Noah's mother dried her eyes. "You've got so much news to catch up on. So many things have happened since your accident."

Noah felt a strange mixture of emotions. He was painfully worried about Harley, and frustrated by his own inability to move. He was afraid that everything around him was a trap. But at the same time, it felt good just to sit and talk with his parents. After weeks of being held prisoner by Umbra, he was more than ready to be home.

"You're going to have to get well fast," his father said, "or you'll miss the rest of the basketball season."

The Doctor cleared his throat. "I'm not sure we're ready to start talking about Noah's fitness for sports in the near future. He will need time to recover, and considerable physical therapy."

"Ah," his father scorned. "My boy will want to get out there and play. Won't you, Noah?"

"Play basketball?" It seemed like an odd thing to say. "The season must be almost over by now."

"No," his father said with a shake of his head. "You've only missed a couple of weeks."

Noah concentrated, doing his best to remember. He had been kidnapped by Umbra near the start of November. By the time he and Harley escaped the cave, it had to be the last week of November, maybe even the start of December. And the Doctor said he had been in the hospital for two months. Even if he and Harley had gone straight back to Stone Harbor, that made it at least February. "What day is it?" he asked.

His mother gave his hand another squeeze. "It's December second, dear."

"December second?" Noah shook his head. "But the Doctor said I had been here two months."

"That's right. You had your accident on the first of October." His mother looked toward the Doctor and spoke in a near whisper. "Does he remember anything?"

"Very little," replied Dr. Ripley. "Though it may come back to him in time."

Noah felt confusion rising so thickly that he barely knew what to say. "I *couldn't* have had my accident in October," he insisted. "That was about the same time the dreams started."

It was his mother's turn to look confused. "What dreams?" she asked.

"The dreams about the aliens," Noah replied.

"Aliens?" Noah's father gave a grunt of surprise. "You never said anything about that nonsense."

Noah turned to his mother, but she only shook her head. "Remember?" he continued. "I started having trouble sleeping, staying up all night. My grades got worse. I got suspended from the team."

"Suspended from the team!" his father exclaimed. "Son, if that had happened I would have heard about it. You were never suspended from the team."

"I *was*," argued Noah. "And then Harley came to town, and the base at Tulley Hill exploded, and I was kidnapped. You have to remember that. I was gone for weeks."

The happy expression on his mother's face gave way to fear. "None of those things happened, Noah."

"They *did*," Noah maintained. "And other things too."

His father shook his head. "Son, for the last two months, you've been in this hospital bed. Either me or your mother has been here every day to see you. You weren't kidnapped, or suspended from the team."

"I *was!*" Noah shouted. To his own embarrassment, Noah felt tears coming close. Now that his emotions had returned, they seemed to have returned stronger than ever.

"Well, if you've been suspended," said a voice from the door. "We better get Coach to let you back on the team. I need a break."

Noah turned as much as he could to look at the figure coming into the room. If seeing his parents had been a surprise, what he was seeing now was purely impossible. "Josh?"

"Hey, you remember my name," said Josh McQuinn. "That proves that all the important parts of your brain survived that knock on your skull."

Noah could only stare. Josh had been his best friend from kindergarten to high school. Not until the very end had Noah discovered that Josh was really a Legion agent, sent to Stone Harbor to watch over Noah's progress. Then Josh's bullet-ridden body had dissolved in a pile of steaming green goo. Josh McQuinn was dead.

Except he wasn't. He was standing in the door of Noah's hospital room, his bone pale hair slicked back and the sleeves of his letterman's jacket pulled halfway to his elbows. He looked as if he were ready to ask out a cheerleader or take a fast ride in his Camaro.

Josh frowned. "Hey, buddy. I thought you'd be glad to see me. What's wrong?"

"Everything," said Noah miserably. "Everything."

"Miss."

Harley awoke instantly. She surged to her feet, her hands raised to ward off a blow.

"Whoa! It's all right, miss. Calm down now."

Harley blinked the sleep out of her eyes. She was standing in front of a simple wooden bench in a broad hallway that was lined with paintings in heavy wooden frames. Standing a few feet away was an elderly man with silvery hair, wire-rimmed glasses, and a worried expression on his face. "Sorry," she said.

The older man smiled. "It's all right. I'm sorry I had to disturb you. But you can't sleep in here."

Embarrassment brought a warmth to Harley's cheeks. After her run in with Braddock and Unit 17, she had been scared to go straight back to the hospital. She was afraid that Unit 17 would follow her to Noah. So she had run along one street after another, pressing her exhausted legs to keep going while she scanned the street for anyone following.

Finally, exhausted and shivering with cold, she had spotted the little art museum. It was a public place, a place where lots of people were going in and out. Harley decided it would be a safe enough spot to stop for a few minutes—just long enough to warm up and work the cramps out of her legs.

"I'm sorry," she said again. "I never meant to fall asleep."

"It's all right," said the elderly man. He leaned in closer and lowered his voice. "There are a number of shelters nearby. Would you like me to place a call for you?"

A fresh flood of embarrassment washed over Harley. She looked down at her clothes, dirty and scorched from her slide down the chute. To the museum worker, she had to look like a street kid. "No, that's all right. I'll just be going."

"Feel free to come back," said the man. "But do try to stay awake."

Harley thanked the man again and hustled out on the street. From the slant of the sunlight between the buildings, she had been inside the museum for far longer than she had intended. She stood in the street for a moment, trying to get her directions straight, then headed for the hospital, where she had left Noah. She hoped that all his tests had gone well and that Noah hadn't gotten tired of waiting.

Harley opened up her dusty backpack and pulled out a couple of bucks. At the next intersection, she went down the long escalator to a metro station and rode the blue line toward the heart of the city. The fast-moving train took her within a few blocks of the hospital at a pace far more rapid than walking.

Several times, Harley looked around her, but she saw no sign she was being followed. She wasn't sure that meant anything. Unit 17 was probably quite capable of surrounding her with a hundred agents all dressed like tourists and businessmen. They might be following her to find Noah, or they might have only been waiting until she was somewhere out of the public eye before making their move. Her only hope was that she had lost them back at the office building

With the sun already so low that it was hidden by the nearby buildings, Harley made it back to the hospital. She walked into the ER cautiously, still looking for Unit 17 soldiers. If anything, the waiting room was even busier than it had been that morning. Dozens of people sat in stiff chairs. A handful of others leaned over a desk and filled out paperwork. She saw no sign of Noah.

A nurse walked quickly across the room with two bags of blood in her hand.

"Excuse me," said Harley. "I'm looking for—"

"Not now," the nurse snapped. She walked on past Harley without slowing.

Harley jogged a couple of steps to keep up. "But I left a friend here. He was hurt and—"

"Check with the desk," the nurse said, cutting Harley off again. She went through a door and shut it pointedly in Harley's face.

Harley scowled at the door for a moment, then went back to the desk. "Excuse me," she started again.

The man behind the desk pointed across the room. "End of the line," he said flatly.

"But all I have is a question," Harley protested.

The man rolled his eyes. "Everybody has a question. Go to the end of the line."

Fuming, Harley went to the place the man had pointed out and stood in line. For ten minutes she waited while people ahead of her asked questions about insurance forms and confusing prescriptions.

Finally, she reached the front of the line. "Now will you answer my question?" she asked.

"Depends. What's the question?"

"I'm looking for my friend, Noah Templer. We came in here together."

"Templer?" The man turned to a computer terminal and typed for a few seconds. "Nope, we don't have one of those." He leaned past Harley. "Next!"

"Wait," said Harley. "Where's my friend?"

"If he's not in the computer, he's not here. Next!" the man called again.

Harley slammed her fist down on the table. "I left a friend here," she said. "I want to know where he is."

The man behind the desk peered at Harley as if she were a form of insect—some particularly unpleasant little bug that had crawled out from under a rock. "Look. I already told you, he's not in the computer. Now, you can look for him yourself, or you can go around to the main desk and annoy them for as long as you want." He leaned back in his chair and picked up the phone. "But if you don't get out of my way, I'm going to call security and have them drag you out of here. Understand?"

Harley ground her teeth together so hard that she could hear her jaw creaking. This was ridiculous. She could smash the secret headquarters of an ancient and powerful organization, she could escape the clutches of a world-spanning paramilitary conspiracy, but she couldn't get past a desk jockey and his brain-dead computer.

She scanned the waiting room. Noah had to be somewhere nearby. He had known Harley was coming back, and even though she was a couple of hours late she didn't think he would have left—unless he was *forced* to leave.

A blond woman stepped past Harley on her way to the door. Harley moved aside to let her by, but as the woman started past, Harley suddenly recognized her. "Wait," she said. "Aren't you Doctor Burris?"

The woman turned. "Yes, I . . ." Her words trailed away and her lips parted in surprise. "Didn't I examine you this morning?"

"Yes," said Harley. "Me, and a friend of mine. We were in an accident."

"I remember." Dr. Burris looked Harley up and down. "What happened to you?" she asked with a touch of sarcasm. "Another accident?"

"You might say that," Harley replied. "But I'm all right. I'm here looking for my friend, Noah."

"He's not with you?" Dr. Burris frowned. "We thought you left together." She leaned in closer. "Billing was having fits. They thought the two of you had taken off before they could get the insurance information."

Harley shook her head. "I left Noah here. You said he needed some more tests and that it was going to take a couple of hours."

The Doctor nodded slowly. "But when I went back to the examining room, you were both gone." She frowned and looked around the crowded room. "Wait here, I'm going to see if someone admitted him into the hospital. It's been a real madhouse around here today."

Harley collapsed gratefully in a chair while she waited for the doctor to return. She closed her eyes and drew in a deep breath. The argument with the desk clerk had left her steaming, but now that Dr.

Burris was taking care of things, her anger was beginning to fade. In its place came fear.

Noah was missing. Again.

Harley wondered what she would do if the Doctor couldn't find him. She was completely on her own, without the help of her father, or Dee, or Scott and Kenyon. And even though she was short of friends, she still had plenty of enemies. For reasons that Harley didn't come close to understanding, Unit 17 wanted the golden orb. Whatever the reason, she was willing to bet that Braddock and his men would not give up easily.

Something nagged at her about the encounter with the Unit 17 commander. She had that unpleasant *tickly* feeling that comes when you've left on a trip and forgotten to pack the one thing you needed most. She had missed something in Braddock's words—something important. Harley played back the conversation in her mind. What Braddock had told her about her father almost had to be a lie. No matter what her father was working on, Harley couldn't see how it could involve transportation. But that wasn't what was bugging her. It was something else, something . . .

She frowned. How had Braddock known where to find her?

It was possible that Unit 17 had located the office building. Scott and Kenyon had been staying there for days, and the FBI raid on the building was bound to have attracted some attention. Maybe Unit 17 had spies watching the place for any sign of Harley or the others. But she had only been in the building for a couple of minutes before Braddock appeared. And Braddock had come from the stairway, not the elevator. It took time to climb twelve floors of stairs. The more Harley thought about it, the more certain she became—Braddock had not followed her to the building, he had been waiting for her there.

Harley didn't believe for a minute that Braddock had been standing around Water Tower Place for days on the chance she might show up. Somehow he had tracked her. Somehow he had known she was coming.

Once again she had the feeling that there was a clue in what the commander had said—some phrase that she should have remembered. Harley wrinkled her forehead in concentration as she tried to recall every word that Braddock had uttered.

And then she had it.

"Scans," she whispered aloud. Braddock had said that his scans showed Harley was carrying the device they were looking for.

She reached into the pouch of her sweatshirt and drew out the golden orb. As usual, the ball was warm to the touch, more like a living thing than a construction of metal. As she held it in her palm, Harley thought she could feel a faint low hum coming from somewhere deep below its gleaming surface.

They knew where I was going because they were watching me, she thought. Unit 17 had devices that could detect the orb. And if they could detect the orb, that meant her escape from the office was only temporary. They could use the same devices to find her again. In fact, it was almost certain that they already *had* found her. At that moment, Unit 17 agents could be watching her, just waiting for the chance to drag her away.

Harley shoved the orb back into her sweatshirt and

glanced quickly around the waiting room. She saw no sign of Dr. Burris. She looked at the people in the other seats. Many of them were elderly. Others held ill children. But there were two men sitting together on the far side of the room that looked suspiciously healthy.

One of the men was quite tall, with the broad, flat chest of an athlete and a hair cut so short it was little more than a dark stubble on his head. He wore heavy brown work boots and held a shiny construction helmet under one arm, but both his boots and helmet were far too clean to have ever seen a construction site. The second man was older, with a heavy, thick body and a blue suit that bulged under his right arm. His face was beefy, with a pinkish scar running between his nose and one corner of his mouth. Harley thought he looked like an advertisement for Thugs 'R' Us.

While Harley was looking at the heavier man, his gaze shifted to meet hers. They looked at each for only a moment, then the man glanced away, apparently searching the magazines on the table next to him. But that brief glance was enough to make Harley sure. The man was an agent.

As casually as she could, Harley got up from her chair. From the corner of her eye she watched the two men as she walked across the room. Both of them raised their heads to watch her pass. Either they were awfully poor spies, or they weren't bothering to hide their interest in her. Harley figured she didn't have long before they made their move.

She ducked into the women's restroom, locked the door, and went straight to the window. The opening was more than big enough to escape through, but it was also locked. No matter how hard Harley shoved the lever holding down the bottom of the window pane, she couldn't get it to move an inch.

There was a knock at the door. "Everything okay in there?" called a deep gravely voice.

Harley's heart jumped in her chest. "Yes," she choked out. "Fine." The voice outside the door might come from some concerned hospital worker, but she doubted it. She looked frantically around the rest room. She found little there, just a soap dispenser, towel rack, and a small metal trash can on the floor. She picked up the trash can and went over to the window.

Someone pounded at the door again. "This restroom is for hospital staff only," said the deep voice. "There's a public restroom just down the hall."

"I'll be done in a second," Harley called. She braced herself, took a deep breath, and swung the trash can as though she was trying to hit the winning home run in a softball game.

The metal can struck the window with a noise like a small car wreck. A spiderweb of cracks appeared in the glass, spreading all the way to the edge of the frame. In the corner of the window a small piece of glass fell away and tinkled on the tile floor of the restroom.

The pounding at the door turned into a heavy thumping. Whoever was outside, they weren't trying to get Harley's attention anymore, they were trying to get in.

She swung again. This time the can crunched through the broken glass, sending jagged fragments flying into the parking lot outside. Behind her one of the hinges on the door let go with a snap.

Harley glanced at the broken window, then at the

door. In a thousandth of a second she made her decision. Instead of swinging the can again, she jumped—trash can and all—into the toilet stall and swung the stall door closed. Once inside, she raised the trash can over her head and waited.

She didn't have to wait long. She heard another heavy impact on the restroom door, and it burst open. Splinters of wood flew from its broken frame and scattered across the floor.

The top of a close-shaven head sped past the toilet stall and stopped beside the shattered window. "She's gone," shouted the false construction worker. "She broke through the window." Another voice answered from the hallway, and Harley heard heavy footsteps thumping away.

Over the top of the stall, Harley watched as the man with the shaven head turned away from the window. Just as he did, she kicked open the stall door and brought the trash can down square in the middle of his forehead.

The metal can rang like a bell. The Unit 17 agent's green eyes rolled back in his head, and he fell to the floor like a stack of loose sticks.

Harley threw the trash can down on top of him. "Next time," she said, "you ought to wear that helmet."

The man on the floor stirred and groaned. He reached out a big hand and grabbed for Harley's ankle. She dodged away and hurried out of the room.

The noise of smashing doors and shattering windows had attracted quite a crowd. Harley stepped into the hallway and found herself facing half a dozen baffled hospital workers and two security guards who looked decidedly unhappy.

"Hold it right there," said one of the guards. "What's going on?"

Harley grabbed him by the sleeve and pulled him toward the door. "Come quick, a man broke into the women's bathroom and started breaking things! He's still in there!"

The two guards pulled out their nightsticks. As they carefully advanced on the shattered bathroom, Harley pushed through the crowd, walked across the waiting room, and slipped out into the parking lot.

She smiled to herself. So far, the Unit 17 agents hadn't seemed too tough.

Then something hard and cold pressed against the base of her neck.

"You'll want to be stopping," said a thin, whispery voice. "That is, if you want to keep your head connected to the rest of you."

A thick hand landed on her shoulder and spun her around. Harley found herself facing the man in the blue suit—and a gun.

"You think you've pretty clever, don't you?" snarled the heavy man.

Harley didn't answer. She was too busy staring at the strange barrel of the gun.

The man waved the weapon toward her face. "Do you know what this is?"

"No," Harley said honestly. She had spent a lifetime on military bases, but she had never seen a gun like this one. It bulked out around the man's hand, then narrowed to a barrel as thin as a pencil. The actual opening at the end of the weapon was nothing but a pinhole.

The man turned the gun aside for a moment and squeezed the trigger. Again Harley heard a sound like a high pitched vacuum cleaner—or like a blender gone mad. From the point of the gun came a line of something that looked like a solid stream of metal. The line reached across the parking lot and touched the base of a hospital sign. Sparks jumped from the metal and the sign twisted and shook as if caught in a hurricane. In less than a second, the post was sheared in half and the sign clattered to the ground. The line of metal stretching out from the gun disappeared and the painful whine died away.

The heavy man turned the tiny barrel back to Harley. "They tell me this thing is called a sliver gun," he said. "From what I understand, it's supposed to fire a stream of hypersonic needles." The man shrugged. "I don't know about that. But I do know what it does to a person. Very messy."

Harley swallowed hard and kept her eyes fixed on the ugly weapon. "I thought Commander Braddock wanted me alive."

"I might have heard something about that," said the heavy man. "Then again, my hearing ain't always so good." He lowered the gun barrel toward Harley's legs. "Besides, you can lose a lot of parts and still live. Understand?"

"Yes," Harley said. She wasn't sure she understood everything the man had said about how the gun worked, but what the weapon could do to her was very clear.

"Now," the man said, "let's get back in there and

collect my stupid partner." He waved the gun toward the door of the hospital.

Harley turned toward the hospital and took a step. Her hand was inches from the handle of the door when she heard a loud scream from inside the hospital, followed by a series of shouts.

The door suddenly burst open. Harley fell and rolled to the side. From the corner of her eye she saw the man she had hit with the trash can come flying through the door at a dead run, blood streaming down his forehead. He smashed right into his partner, and the two men went down in a heap. The black gun flew out of the heavy man's hand and clattered across the parking lot.

For a moment, Harley thought about going for the gun, but the two cursing men were between her and the weapon, and they were already getting on their feet. Instead, Harley stood up and zipped between two parked ambulances. Ten steps later she turned hard right, putting another row of vehicles between herself and the men. Then she shot around the corner of the hospital, jumped past a statue of an angel, and ran down the sidewalk as fast as her legs could carry her.

Usually, that was pretty fast. Harley had been the best distance runner on the girl's track team at every school she had ever attended. At her best, she could do a mile in just over four minutes. But she was a long way from her best. Her legs were bruised, battered, and just plain tired. By the time she had gone half a block, she was already breathing hard. Behind her, she heard the distant thump of boots as one of the Unit 17 agents ran to catch her.

A squeal of brakes drew Harley's attention to the

street. A blue van skidded to a halt in the middle of traffic. Horns blared up and down the block as drivers swerved to avoid the sudden obstacle. Slowly, then with increasing speed, the van cut across lanes of traffic. It was aiming straight for Harley.

She gritted her teeth and ran for all she was worth. Behind her the thump of footsteps was growing closer. But there was a metro station ahead. If she could only make it one more block, she hoped she could lose herself in the confusion of crowds and trains.

She didn't get the chance. The blue van finished crossing the traffic and drove along beside Harley for a dozen strides before plowing up onto the sidewalk right in front of her.

Harley could barely stop in time to keep from running into the van. She stood in the street with the icy air burning in her lungs and looked desperately around for some other chance of escape. She saw none. The agent was fifty feet behind and coming fast, and the van blocked the route ahead. Slowly Harley raised her hands. "All right," she said dejectedly. "Come and get me."

The back door of the van popped open and a round face topped with auburn hair peeked out. "Harley?"

Harley felt her mouth drop open, but she could do nothing to stop it. "Dee? How did you get here?"

"I'll tell you that after you get in," replied Dee. "That is, unless you *want* that guy behind you to catch up."

Harley glanced back. "Right," she said. She reached out a hand to Dee and climbed into the van. With a squeal of tires, they roared away, leaving the hospital—and Noah—behind.

Noah Templer found himself in a place that was both terrible and familiar.

He was in a huge dark room, with the walls lost in distant shadow, and the ceiling out of sight above. Even the floor was invisible. The only light in the room hung above Noah, casting a brilliant circle around the bare metal table on which he lay.

From the corners of the room, the aliens gathered. They moved like ghosts through the darkness, glowing white, with empty black eyes. Four of them appeared. Another four followed close behind. They drew closer to the table. Noah's heart raced in terror as he stared into their lifeless eyes. One of the glowing figures reached out a thin arm. Spidery fingers extended down toward his chest.

The tips of the finger tingled against Noah's bare skin for a moment, then the fingers pushed inside him. Noah could feel their touch moving through flesh and bone. A cold grip settled around his heart, trapping it like an animal in a cage. Slowly, the fingers began to squeeze.

"Noah!" cried a voice. "Noah, wake up!"

He jerked awake. His heartbeat was thumping in his ears and his face was covered in cold sweat. He raised his head and looked around.

The room was light blue, not dark. Noah saw flowers on the bedside table and sun shining through the windows. He was in Westerberg Hospital. Gradually his pounding heart began to slow.

"Was it another dream?"

Noah turned and saw his mother sitting in the chair beside his bed. "Yes," he said, his own voice thick with sleep. "A bad dream. Thanks for waking me."

His mother smiled nervously. She looked older than Noah remembered, and more worn down. Her hair, usually perfectly styled, was loose and carelessly piled on her head. There were new lines at the corners of her eyes and around her mouth.

It had to be hard on her, Noah thought, watching me lie here for weeks.

But on a deeper level, he knew it wasn't true. His mother hadn't sat by his bedside for weeks, because he hadn't *been* in the bed for weeks.

If he was to believe the story his parents had told him, then he had never been kidnapped by Umbra. He had never been betrayed by a girl calling herself Billie, and had never fought with men who seemed to be made from shadow. Tulley Hill Military Base had not exploded. Josh McQuinn was alive and well. There was no world-spanning conspiracy or network of secret societies.

And Harley Davisidaro did not exist.

Noah couldn't believe that. He might believe that some of his memories were wrong. There were plenty of things about the last few weeks that he would have loved to think were nothing but a nightmare—a long and twisted coma dream. But he would never believe that Harley wasn't real.

"Maybe I should tell the nurse," suggested Noah's

mother. "She could bring you something to keep you from having these nightmares."

"No. I'll be okay." Noah pushed himself up in a sitting position.

From the angle of the sun coming through the windows, it was morning again. That made it three days since he had first woken up from his coma. The funny thing was, it didn't feel like three days. Noah had been drowsy most of the time, and several times he had fallen asleep, but it still seemed like no more than a few hours.

His mother reached out and touched him on the cheek. "It looks like your arms are doing better."

"Yes," Noah agreed. Each time he awoke, his body had recovered a little more. Now he seemed to have all strength back in his arms. Some motion was returning to his legs as well. Noah could wiggle his toes, and even turn his feet slightly at the ankles. He couldn't move his knees yet, but he felt sure he'd be able to do that soon.

"Oh," said his mother. "Did I tell you I talked to Caroline this morning?"

"Caroline?"

"Caroline March! Your *girlfriend.*"

Noah remembered Caroline. She was a cheerleader for the basketball team, and she and Noah had dated for months. But when Noah had started having his dreams of alien abduction, he had become so distracted he had lost his spot on the basketball team. Soon afterward, he had made the mistake of telling Caroline about the dreams. Instead of being sympathetic, Caroline had laughed at him. Later, Noah had discovered that Caroline was an agent of Unit 17. Like Josh, Caroline had died in the battle for the base—crushed beneath falling metal.

But supposedly none of that had happened. In the story Noah had learned from his parents and Josh, he and Caroline had still been dating when he had his accident. Caroline was still his girlfriend.

"What does she want?" Noah asked grumpily.

"She wants to come out and see you, Noah," said his mother. "She wants to know why you haven't asked to see her."

Noah stayed silent. He wanted to say that seeing Caroline would be like betraying Harley, something he had done one too many times already, with Billie. Noah and Harley had never really dated—things had always been too crazy for them to get involved in that way—but in every other way, Noah felt closer to Harley than he had to any person he had ever met.

"You're not still thinking about this girl from your dreams?" asked his mother. "What was her name? Carlie?"

"Harley." Noah corrected.

"Harley." His mother leaned forward and patted his hand. "She's not real, Noah. I know she must have seemed real, but she was only part of a dream."

"It couldn't *all* be a dream," Noah insisted. He let an edge of frustration and anger creep into his voice as he reached out to grab the covers at the side of the bed. "*This* is what's fake. This whole place is fake."

His mother sighed. "I know your dreams must have seemed real to you, honey, but just think about what you've told us. I mean, monsters and flying balls of light and secret agents everywhere. How could any of that be real?"

Sitting in the warm bed in the sunny hospital room, Noah's memories of the last two months did seem incredible. All the things that had happened with Umbra and Unit 17 and Legion were so strange, that if anyone had told him about them six months ago, Noah would have thought they were crazy. Looking back on his memories, they did start to seem like part of some long, fever dream.

But Noah wasn't ready to throw those memories away and believe what he was being told. Part of the reason he didn't give in was because he couldn't forget Harley. But there were other reasons, darker reasons, which made him wonder if he could trust his own parents.

The Umbra agent, Billie, had come to Stone Harbor pretending to be another victim of the secret organizations. She had lied to Noah about almost everything, but her lies had sounded convincing, and Noah had believed her. He had believed her so much that he had given her his trust—and part of his heart—only to have his faith crushed when Billie's true motives were revealed.

The most painful thing that Billie had said was about Noah's parents. According to Billie, Noah's parents were agents for the group called Legion.

Noah didn't know if that was true, or if it was just another of Billie's many lies. Sitting in a cell in Umbra's headquarters, he had thought about that statement many times. In a lot of ways, it made sense.

Noah's father had been a poor, struggling fisherman before Noah was born. Within days of Noah's birth, his father had sold his boat and invested in a real estate deal. The deal had paid off spectacularly, turning Noah's father in a rich man overnight. Noah had *always* been suspicious of that million-dollar deal. His father had never seemed like a finical wizard. Was it only coincidence that he had made a lot of money about the time that Noah had been born, or was it a payoff?

Noah had never thought he looked anything like his parents. He was tall and blond, while both of them were shorter and darker. Back at the battle that had destroyed the Tulley Hill base, a dying Josh McQuinn had told Noah that he was the product of a breeding program run by Legion. What if the people that had raised him were not his parents? What if his father's sudden wealth had not come from a real estate deal, but from Legion? The organization might have paid his parents to take him in and raise him as their own.

The woman at his bedside pulled out a handkerchief and dabbed at her eyes. She looked up at Noah and smiled for a moment. Her smile vanished and was replaced by a puzzled expression. "What's wrong?"

"Nothing," Noah replied. "Nothing's wrong."

The woman he had called mother all his life shook her head. "You were looking at me so oddly, Noah. Are you sure you're feeling all right?"

"I'm fine . . . Mom." Noah's throat tightened. If he believed his parents, then Harley was only a figment of his imagination. If he refused to believe them, then his parents had never really been his parents. His whole *life* was nothing but an illusion.

"Do you want me to bring you something to eat?" asked his mother.

Noah shook his head. "I'm feeling tired. I think I'll sleep a little more."

His mother nodded. "All right, Noah. I would have thought you had slept enough by now, but Doctor Ripley told us you might feel tired for a few days."

Noah looked into the woman's weary eyes. "Why don't you go home and get some rest yourself?"

"Oh, no," she said with a shake of her head. "I should stay close by."

"I'll be fine." Noah worked up a smile he hoped was convincing. "I've got the nurses if I need anything. You need to get your rest so you'll be ready to celebrate when I come—" Noah's voice cracked, and he had to draw another breath before finishing the sentence. "—when I come home."

His mother hesitated for a moment, then nodded. "I *could* do with a little sleep," she admitted. "But I'll be back out here later. All right?"

"That's fine," said Noah. "You get some sleep."

"Oh, Noah." His mother reached in and grabbed his hand. She squeezed so hard her fingers dug into his palm. "You don't know how good it is to see you getting better. If we had lost you, I don't know what I would have done." She released Noah's hand, wiped another tear from her face, and hurried out of the room.

Noah stared at the door for minutes after she left. He felt like he was being torn in half. Part of him desperately wanted to believe in the world his parents described. He wanted to go back to being a normal high-school student, to play basketball, to take chemistry exams, and to wonder what movie he would take Caroline to see on Friday night. But the other half of him was certain that the things he had been through in the last weeks were real.

As he lay there trying to think of some way to decide, Noah found that he really was becoming tired. He lay his head back on his pillow and closed his eyes. The world behind Noah's eyelids seemed barren and empty. The torture that Umbra put him through had been terrible at the time, but the powers he had gained had almost been worth it. Now those powers were gone.

He felt that if he could only climb the slender thread leading up to the nexus, everything would become clear. He could hang in the empty space between people's dreams, letting his own mind grow calm. He could search for Harley among the threads, and prove to himself that she was real. If he only had his powers.

A shadow of doubt began to creep into Noah's mind. Maybe the powers were gone because they had never really been there at all. The nexus, and the threads, and the ability to see flashes of past and future had all been missing when he first had awakened in the hospital room. If those abilities were all just part of the dream, then it made sense that they would go away when he woke up.

Noah's heart began to race in his chest. What if they *were* telling the truth? What if there really were no mysterious groups and no secret war? What if Harley Davisidaro was nothing but a figment of his imagination?

His thoughts were interrupted by a faint metallic click from somewhere close by.

Noah opened his eyes to find himself immersed in a vast black room. The warm bed had become a bare metal table. The sunny room was replaced by a empty space lit by a single harsh light somewhere high overhead. And from the shadows, the aliens gathered.

It's a dream, Noah told himself firmly. I've fallen asleep again, and this is nothing but another dream.

The swollen white faces circled around Noah, always moving. They leaned over him one moment, then drew back. One of the aliens surged forward, its wire-thin glowing fingers stretching toward Noah's face. Noah wished he could at least close his eyes. He didn't want to see those colorless fingers reaching into his flesh.

"Stay back!" commanded a voice from the darkness.

Silently, the aliens gave ground. They moved back ten feet from the side of the metal slab, but they continued to circle and reach their grasping hands toward Noah.

A new figure emerged from the darkness. This time it was a man, dressed in a white coat with crisp formal clothes underneath. The heels of his shoes clicked against the unseen floor. As the man stepped closer, Noah recognized the odd yellow hair and angular face of Dr. Ripley. For a moment, Noah was glad to see the Doctor. The man had kept the aliens away from Noah, and that was certainly good. But the closer Doctor Ripley got to Noah, the stranger the expression on his face seemed. Something about the Doctor—an air of tension and violence—was almost as frightening as the aliens.

"Keep clear of him," Dr. Ripley warned the circling figures.

One of the white forms raised its arms toward the Doctor, and Noah heard a thin rattling whisper like leaves being blown along an autumn street.

"No," Ripley replied to the creature. "Don't be a fool. We're not done with the preparations."

The Doctor stepped past the circling aliens and walked to the side of Noah's bed. He pulled a curved metal rod from the pocket of his jacket and held it above the bed. After a moment, a haze of blue static gathered around the rod. The cloud of electricity spread into the air, and a handful of long sparks arced down to strike the metal bed with sharp snaps. With each bolt, Noah's arms and legs jumped and twitched. The bitter scent of ozone burned his nose. Finally, the Doctor ran his other hand along the rod, brushing the electricity away like dust, and returned the strange instrument to his pocket.

"The new barriers are holding," said Dr. Ripley, "but we can't tell for how long."

Another of the white figures spoke like a sandstorm hissing against a window.

Ripley seemed to understand its speech. "That's true," he replied. "But that was before he tasted freedom. He's no longer so easily restrained." The Doctor looked down at Noah and rubbed his chin. "We have two days, perhaps three, to complete the transference. Otherwise, he may free himself from our grip."

The Doctor reached into his pocket again and came out with a syringe. It looked much like the kind of syringe that was used for giving flu shots, only the needle at the end of this syringe was a good three inches long and the fluid inside glowed a hard, poisonous green. Dr. Ripley raised the glowing syringe and inspected its contents. He made a slight adjustment, spilling a pair of glowing drops onto the table. Then he turned the syringe over and lowered the point toward Noah's face.

It's a dream, Noah chanted in his mind as the tip of the needle neared his left eye. It's only a dream.

But deep inside, he didn't believe it was a dream any more than he believed he had spent the last two months lying in a cozy bed in a sunny room. From far down inside, a burst of anger and fear surged upward, driving the paralysis from Noah's body.

Noah's right hand felt as if it were tied down by a hundred pound weight, but he raised it from the table, pulled it back, and slapped the syringe from the Doctor's hand.

Dr. Ripley's sharp face froze in shock. "How—" he began.

"Get. Away. From. Me," demanded Noah, forcing each word out between his clenched teeth.

The Doctor stumbled back a step. The white figures raised their arms and shrieked like a gale blowing over the mouth of a hundred empty bottles.

And then the world fell apart.

Slabs of color and ribbons of light went spinning around Noah's head. His ears were filled with the sound of car horns and seagulls and an aluminum baseball bat pounding out a home run. He tasted mustard and hot fudge and turpentine. Fire and ice, feathers and razors, chased themselves across his skin. From the chaos whirled square walls of light blue and a machine that beeped and a man in a white coat.

Noah was back in his bed in Westerberg Hospital. At the foot of the bed stood Dr. Ripley with a chart in his hands.

"I see you're awake again," said the Doctor. He smiled at Noah. "How are you feeling?"

Noah looked up at the Doctor and fought back a scream. "Fine," he choked out. "I'm just fine."

"That's good," said the Doctor. He dropped the clipboard into a holder at the end of the bed. "Well, I better get on with my rounds. Get your rest."

"I will."

Noah watched the Doctor vanish through the door, then he quickly closed his eyes. At first he saw nothing, but after moments of tense concentration, a faint glow appeared in the hallway.

It's real. All of my memories are real.

He opened his eyes again. He saw little, just a hospital room with blue walls, and sun shining through the windows. But for a fraction of a second, Noah was sure he spotted something small and white and skeleton-thin scuttling away down the hall.

SIX

"Are we ever going to stop?" asked Harley.

"Not until I'm satisfied that we're not being followed," Kenyon Moor said from the driver's seat of the van.

Dee Janes laughed. "Then I guess we'll never stop," she said, "because he's never satisfied with *anything*."

Kenyon turned from his seat for a moment and sent Dee a dark look. "As long as you're around, there's very little to be satisfied about," he snipped. He turned back to watch the traffic.

Harley looked at them and shook her head. "It's certainly good to see that the two of you are getting along as well as always."

"Oh, yeah," said Dee. "We go together like mashed potatoes and caviar."

Harley raised her chin and squinted toward the front of the van. The passenger seat was empty. "Where's Scott?"

"He's back at the new place," explained Dee. She smiled. "Wait till you see it. You're going to love it."

Harley dragged her aching body across the van and sat beside Dee. "I still don't understand," she said. "How did you find me?"

"Radio," Kenyon said from the front of the van.

"Hey," Dee called. "Are you going to drive or talk?" She looked over at Harley. "Scott rigged some kind of special radio. It's kind of like a police band, but the people we've been listening to sure aren't the police."

78

"Unit 17?" asked Harley.

Dee nodded, her auburn hair swinging around her face. "That's what we think. We heard them talking about Water Tower Place this afternoon, but they were gone before we could get near. Then we heard a signal calling everyone to the old city hospital, so we zipped over there and—tah dah!—we grabbed you just in the nick of time."

"I'm sure glad you did." Harley reached over, put an arm around the smaller girl's shoulders, and gave her a quick hug. "That's the second time you've saved my life."

Dee grinned at her. "Is it only two?"

"What about Noah?" Harley asked. "Do you know what they've done with him?"

Dee's smile faded quickly. "No, we haven't seen Noah since we left you guys back at Water Tower Place the day before yesterday. We were hoping he was with you."

Harley brushed her hair out of her face and watched the lights of the city swing by outside the van's windows. "He is with me," she said. "Or at least, he was until this morning. Noah got hurt while we were escaping from Umbra. I left him at the hospital while I went to look for you guys. When I got back, he was gone and Unit 17 was waiting."

"They must have taken him," said Dee. "Don't worry. We'll find him again."

Harley sighed. "I hope so." She felt a touch of both sadness and anger. If she ever got both Noah and her father back at the same time, Harley decided she was going to superglue them both to the ground before anyone could kidnap them again.

As the van drove on for long minutes, Harley's

exhaustion caught up with her. She closed her eyes and drowsed while Kenyon steered up one street and down the next in a pattern only he understood.

"All right," Kenyon announced at last. "It looks like no one is tailing us. I'm going to head for home."

"That's good," Harley said sleepily. Then a little alarm went off in her mind and she sat bolt upright. "Wait! You can't do that."

"Why not?"

Harley fished into her sweatshirt and came out with the golden orb. "I think we might have a problem," she warned.

Dee leaned in close to the orb. "Cool," she said. "What is it?"

"I'm not sure," admitted Harley. "I picked it up in Umbra's cave."

"*Where?*" Dee asked.

Harley shook her head. "I'll explain later." She raised her voice and called toward the front of the van. "The problem is, I think they might be able to track me."

Kenyon stomped on the brakes and steered the van to the side of the road. In a moment, he had climbed out of the driver's seat and was standing over Harley. He wore a black turtleneck and dark jeans. "What do you *mean* they can track you?" he asked in a cold voice.

"Not me, exactly. I think they can track this." Harley held up the orb for him to see. "It's something Umbra used, and now Unit 17 seems to want it."

Kenyon bent down and studied the metal ball. His clean, handsome features were expressionless as he stared at the orb. "So this is the device," he said softly.

"You knew about it?" Harley asked in surprise.

"I knew there *was* a device," said Kenyon. "I heard the Unit 17 agents talking about it on the radio. But I didn't know what it looked like. You're right about one thing—they want it. They want it very badly." He stared at the sphere for a moment longer, then held out his hand. "Give it to me."

Harley hesitated for a second. Deep inside a voice insisted that the sphere was hers. After all, she had found it. She pushed the voice away and put the ball in Kenyon's hand. "Be careful with it," she cautioned.

Kenyon moved his hand up and down, obviously testing the weight of the orb. "It's not gold," he said. "Or if it is, then it's mostly hollow."

Dee gave another quick laugh. "Did you think Unit 17 wanted it because it would make a great necklace?"

Kenyon ignored her. "If you're right about them tracking this device, then we'll have to find some way to block whatever they're using to pick up its signal."

"But how?" asked Harley. "We don't even know how Unit 17 is tracking it."

For a moment, all three of them were silent. Then Dee snapped her fingers. "What about six inches of solid steel? Would that keep Unit 17 from peeking in?"

"I don't know," said Harley. "What do you mean?"

"A safe," explained Dee. "There's a safe back at the new headquarters. We pop it in there, slam the door, and let Braddock and crew wander around all they want."

Harley thought about it. No matter how Unit 17 was detecting the sphere, she didn't see how they could find it inside a safe. "It sounds great," she said. "Let's go."

"No," said Kenyon.

"What do you mean no?" said Harley.

"I mean you can't take this back to the headquarters." He examined the orb for a moment longer, then returned it to Harley. "We don't know if the safe will really keep Unit 17 from finding the device. I'm not taking it back to headquarters until we can be sure."

Harley looked up at him and scowled. "What would *you* suggest instead?"

"We take it somewhere else," said Kenyon. "We can take it to a bank and leave it in a deposit box."

"No," said Harley.

Kenyon's dark eyes widened. "What?"

"You heard me." Harley climbed to her feet and stared into his face. "Unit 17 wants this thing bad enough to risk being caught in public. Now, I don't know what it can do, but I know I'm not going to leave it someplace where I can't watch it. Where the orb goes, I go."

There was a tense silence as Kenyon returned Harley's glare. "All right," he said slowly. "The orb goes with us." He went back to the front of the van, shoved the vehicle into gear, and steered out into traffic.

Harley collapsed onto the floor next to Dee and let out a sigh of relief.

Dee leaned in close to Harley's ear. "It must be love," she whispered. "He would never have given in if I was the one doing the asking."

"No," Harley told Dee quietly. "It wasn't love that made him agree. It was hate." She looked toward the front of the van where the top of Kenyon's head was just visible above the back of the driver's seat. "Unit 17 killed his parents. If they come after the orb, that'll just give him another chance to get back at them."

It took another twenty minutes for the van to reach their destination. Kenyon turned down a narrow alley, pulled into a parking slot only inches bigger than the van, and killed the engine. "Everybody out," he said. "Let's get that ball into the safe as fast as we can."

Harley followed the others to a door at the back of the building. Kenyon produced a key, turned it in a lock, and waved Harley inside. She stepped into a hallway lined with dark cherry wood paneling on the walls and rich scarlet carpet underfoot. Small crystal chandeliers dotted the ceiling, casting warm pools of yellow light.

"What is this place?"

"The Royal Ambassador Hotel," replied Kenyon. He closed the door and locked it behind them. "Come on. The elevator's at the other end of the hall."

Dee walked along at Harley's side. "You're not going to believe this place," she said.

The elevator itself was a collection of gleaming mirrors and polished brass. When it opened onto the nineteenth floor, Harley found herself staring in wonder. The entire floor was all one suite. It was huge, big enough to play full-court basketball. She saw a grand piano in one corner surrounded by a half circle of plush chairs. In another part of the vast room, a fire crackled merrily in a fireplace.

"This is spectacular," Harley said. "You could put

every house I ever lived in inside this place and still have room left over."

"Yeah, I guess sometimes it pays to have a gazillionaire on your side," Dee admitted.

Kenyon only shrugged. "The furniture is all reproductions," he said, waving a hand. "But it is comfortable."

Scott Handleson emerged from a door at the far side of the room. He was tall and thin, with a blond ponytail swinging behind his head. While Kenyon always seemed to be frowning, Scott generally wore a smile. As soon as he saw Harley, his face lit up. "They found you!" he shouted. He crossed the big penthouse with a dozen fast steps and wrapped his long, thin arms around Harley. "We've been so worried."

Harley let herself lean against Scott's tall frame. "I was worried about you guys too."

"Hey," said Dee. "Over here."

Scott removed his arms from Harley and bent down to wrap Dee in a tight hug. Then he kissed her. "I missed you too," he said.

Even before she and Noah had been captured by Umbra, Harley had noticed that Dee and Scott were getting to be very close. The tall, gangly Scott and the short Dee didn't look like they fit together, but they had a good sense of humor in common. From the way Scott held on to Dee, it was obvious their relationship had deepened while Harley was away.

"The orb," Kenyon said. "We need to get it into the safe."

"Oh, right." Harley pulled out the golden ball

and followed Kenyon across the spacious penthouse. Under a delicate Chinese vase was a metal safe painted to match the nearby furniture.

Kenyon knelt down on the floor and gave the knob at the front of the safe a few quick twists. The heavy door swung open soundlessly. "All right," he said. "Put it inside."

"Hang on a second," Scott called from across the room. He loped over to Harley and squinted at the metal ball. "Is this thing the device those guys on the radio have been slobbering about?"

Harley nodded. "This is it."

Scott bent down close to Harley's hand and peered at the orb. "No evident controls. It looks like an alloy. Not bronze." He stroked his long chin. "Maybe some rare earths. Or something like electrum. Is it heavy?"

"No," said Harley. "You want to hold it?"

Scott took the ball from her and turned it over slowly between. "I don't see any way to open it."

"As far as I know, it doesn't open," Harley told him. "It's just a ball."

Kenyon cleared his throat. "It's a ball that Unit 17 can detect. We need to put it into the safe before we have a hundred agents knocking down our door."

Scott rolled the ball over a few more times then handed it back to Harley. "I wish we had some more equipment," he said. "I'd love to know what's inside that thing."

"All that matters now is getting it out of sight," Kenyon insisted. "Put it in the safe."

Harley bent to put the orb in the safe, and was surprised to see that the first shelf held a pair of ugly black pistols and four more devices that looked like a mad cross between a hand drill and a car battery. "What are those?"

"Glock 9 millimeters up front," said Kenyon. "T-77 Tasers in the back."

"What are you going to use those for?"

Kenyon sighed. "The next time someone shoots at me, I intend to shoot back. The Tasers are for when I want the person I'm shooting at to be able to tell me something after they're down." He reached in and ran a finger along the dark barrel of one of the pistols. "The Glocks are for when I don't care. Now, will you *please* put that thing inside the safe?"

Harley shoved the golden orb onto a soft velvet cloth beside the guns. As soon as her arm was out of the way, Kenyon swung the door shut and spun the dial. "There," he said. "Now we can only hope that stops Unit 17 from detecting it."

"You're counting on the *safe* to block whatever they're using to detect it?" asked Scott.

Harley nodded. "Don't you think it will?"

"It might," Scott said with a shrug. "But we can do better than that."

"How?" asked Kenyon.

Scott gestured toward the safe. "I'll run some wire around it and make a Faraday cage."

"A *what?*" Harley asked, blinking at Scott.

"A Faraday cage. Most of the time, they're used to protect computer systems from outside radiation." He waved his long arms. "Nuclear explosions.

Electromagnetic pulse. That sort of thing."

Harley wasn't sure she understood half of what Scott had just said. "Does that mean it can stop Unit 17 from finding the orb?"

He nodded. "They've got to be tracking it with some form of EM radiation. If I bottle it up right, nothing will get out for them to detect."

Dee walked over and put an arm around Scott's waist. "Pretty cool, huh?" she said with a smile.

"Yeah," Harley agreed. "Pretty cool."

While Scott worked to prevent the orb from being detected, Harley, Kenyon, and Dee took seats in front of the crackling fire. In bits and pieces, they exchanged the events of the last three days.

"We saw you guys being taken out of the building," said Dee. "We even tried to follow you, but the building they took you to was loaded with FBI agents."

Harley nodded. "It was the real FBI that came for me and Noah, but it wasn't the FBI running the operation—it was Billie."

"Billie?" Dee scowled. "It figures she would turn up again. Where did you guys go after that? We lost your trail from there."

Harley explained as best she could about Umbra's headquarters and about the new abilities that Noah had gained. She made her report as fast and as simple as possible, but the story took some time to tell. Finally, she discussed the battle in the cavern, their long dark hike through the lightless caves, and their return to Washington.

When she finished, Dee was looking at her with

wide eyes. "I can't believe you guys lived through all that," she said. "What was the thing in the pit?"

Harley started to answer, but Kenyon cut her off. "It was obviously nothing more than an illusion," he said bluntly.

"It was real enough," Harley pronounced. "I don't know what it was, but it was real."

Kenyon snorted. "A giant monster living in a pit of fire. What else did you see? Little devils with pitchforks?"

Harley started to snap back at him, but instead she only shook her head. "I'm too tired to argue with you," she said. "You can believe whatever you want, but it was real."

The expression on Kenyon's face made it clear enough that he believed very little of Harley's story. "What about Unit 17?" he asked. "How did you know they were after your little metal tennis ball?"

"I went back to Water Tower Place looking for you," Harley explained. Suddenly she remembered the picture of Kenyon and his family she had found. "Oh, hey," she said, as she dug the photo out of her pocket and then handed it over to Kenyon. "I guess you left this there."

Kenyon took the photograph from Harley's hand, stared at it a moment with an unreadable expression on his face, and then slipped it into his shirt pocket. "Thank you," he told Harley softly.

"Is that your little brother?" she asked.

Kenyon immediately stiffened. "I don't want to talk about him," he said flatly.

Harley shrugged. If he wanted to talk about his

family, he would. Until then, Kenyon could keep any secrets he wanted—as long as they didn't put her into any danger.

"So what happened when you got to Water Tower Place?" Scott prompted.

"Oh," Harley continued. "Commander Braddock was waiting there for me. He tried to catch me, but I got away by sliding down a big tube hanging from the side of the building."

"That's a disposal chute," said Kenyon. "It lets the work crew dispose of broken lumber and scraps of plaster board without going up and down the elevator a thousand times a day." His eyes narrowed. "That chute was attached to the eighth floor."

Harley nodded. "Yeah, that's right."

"Are you telling me you jumped into a disposal chute eight stories above the ground?"

"Compared to letting Unit 17 catch me, it seemed like a good idea," Harley replied.

Kenyon shook his head in amazement. "Either you're very brave, or completely nuts." He got out of his chair and walked over to join Scott by the safe.

Dee dragged her chair closer to Harley. "See," she said, looking across the room at Kenyon. "It must be love. He never says anything like that to me or Scott."

Harley laughed. "Kenyon doesn't like me. We never do anything but argue."

"You didn't see him while you were gone," Dee whispered. "He was absolutely *insane*. I don't think he's slept since he found out you were missing."

Harley turned and looked across the room.

Kenyon was bent down beside the safe, cutting lengths of electrical wiring from a long roll. He moved with a confidence and energy that was attractive, and there was no doubt he was handsome, but the idea that Kenyon might like her struck Harley as one of the strangest of the strange things that happened over the last weeks. "That sweater he's wearing probably cost more than my dad's car."

"Don't knock it," Dee said. She leaned back in the plush chair. "Having money never hurts."

"I don't know about that." Harley glanced around the huge penthouse. It seemed almost as alien to her as Umbra's underground base. "I think it would do Kenyon good to try being poor for a while."

"Maybe once you're married you can take the checkbook away from him," Dee suggested.

Harley groaned. Talking to Dee about Kenyon was fun, but it made Harley feel uncomfortable—because of her feelings for Noah, she supposed. Whatever *those* were, exactly. "Please don't start," she told Dee.

Dee stood up. "I'm going over to see if I can help. There's a big stock of food in the kitchen if you want anything."

"No thanks," Harley replied. "I think I'll just sit here and rest awhile."

With the fire warming her feet, Harley relaxed into the chair and closed her eyes. In moments, she drifted into sleep. But her sleep was not comfortable or quiet. It was filled with jagged fragments of dreams and snatches of nightmare. She saw her father standing before a glowing ball of light a monstrous impossible creature climbing up from the flaming heart of the world Commander Braddock laughing in his blue Unit 17 uniform, and Noah laying in some dark place.

When she awoke a few hours later, Harley's neck was stiff and her mouth was filled with the stale taste of sleep. Her legs and arms ached terribly.

"Hi," said a soft voice.

Harley turned her head and saw Scott sitting in one of the other chairs. A strange expression was on his face. "Hi," she answered. "What's up?"

"Dee told me you were taken by Umbra," said the tall boy.

"Yeah. We were in their headquarters."

Scott bit his lip. "While you were there, did you see a girl? She's about sixteen. Small, with curly blond hair."

Harley felt a twinge of guilt. "Chloe?"

Scott nodded. "Did you see her?"

Chloe had been with Scott at an orphanage when he was young. They had been as close as brother and sister, and when Chloe disappeared, Scott had traced her to Umbra. Harley would have loved to give him good news about his missing friend, but she could only shake her head. "I'm sorry," she said. "I didn't see anyone down there but me, Noah, Umbra agents—and a bunch of nasty creatures I don't want to think about."

A frown darkened Scott's usually sunny features. He nodded slowly. "That's all right," he said. "We'll find her."

"Yes," said Harley, trying to sound as certain as she could. "I'm sure we will."

Scott got up and walked away. Harley leaned into the soft chair, and was almost asleep when she heard her name from across the room.

"From what they said on the radio, they're still looking for Harley."

Harley turned her head and saw that the others were gathered around a small glass table. Soft drinks and snacks lay scattered between them. Whatever they were discussing, it had to be serious, because even Dee was frowning.

Kenyon picked up a cola, took a sip, then wiped his mouth. "I don't like the idea of running," he said.

"What good are we doing here?" Scott asked. "We don't have any more leads. All we can do is listen in on the radio."

"They might get sloppy," said Kenyon. "I don't think they've realized we're listening in. They might reveal the location of their own base."

"And what if they do?" asked Dee. "Are we going to raid a base full of soldiers armed with weirdo weapons?"

Harley climbed stiffly from her chair and limped over to the table. "What are you guys up to?"

"We're trying to reach a decision," Kenyon answered gruffly. "The way we see it, the choices are to stay here and hope Unit 17 makes a mistake, or to leave town and get safely out of their sight."

"Leave town?" Harley frowned. "Why would you want to leave town?"

Scott spoke up. "If we get away from town, I

might be able to study the device you brought without Unit 17 detecting us. If we learn how it works, we can use it against them."

"So," said Kenyon. "Those are the choices: wait here, or leave. What do you think?"

Harley was surprised that Kenyon would ask her opinion. "I don't think we should do either one."

Kenyon raised a dark eyebrow. "And just what do you think we should do instead?"

Harley walked over to the table, pulled out the remaining chair, and sat down with the others. She was silent for a moment, organizing her thoughts. "I can't leave town," she said at last, "because Noah is somewhere nearby."

"How do you know?" asked Kenyon. "If Unit 17 has him, they could have taken him anywhere by now."

"He's nearby," insisted Harley. "I can't tell you how I know, I just know."

"Then you vote to wait and see what happens."

"No." Harley shook her head. "I don't want to wait for them to do something. I vote we do something ourselves."

Dee grinned. "Cool. What do you want to do?"

Harley shrugged. "All these organizations have been kidnapping us and our friends and families. Let's see how *they* like it."

Kenyon frowned. "What are you saying?"

Harley picked up a soda, popped the tab, and took a long drink before answering. She thumped the can down on the glass table.

"I'm saying we should kidnap Commander Braddock," she replied.

S
E
V
E
N

"Hey, buddy. You awake?"

Noah opened his eyes to find Josh McQuinn looking down at him. "Yeah," he said. "I'm up."

Josh dropped into the chair beside Noah's bed. "So, how's it going?" he asked.

Noah pushed himself up into a sitting position. "It's going all right," he replied. He forced a smile. Sure, he thought to himself. Except for the fact that you're dead, my parents are lying to me, and aliens keep sticking their hands through my skin, everything's going just great.

"You ready to get out of that bed?" Josh reached out and punched Noah in the arm, "How about going one-on-one?"

"I don't think I'm quite ready for that."

"Yeah, well." Josh leaned back in his chair and flipped up the collar of his letterman's jacket. "You never *were* ready for me."

Noah frowned. Josh was so *Josh*. He looked the same, talked the same, and had all the same movements. But Noah had seen Josh shot dead at the Tulley Hill base. He had seen Josh's dead body dissolve into green slime on the blacktop. Whoever was sitting in the chair beside the bed, it couldn't be Josh.

"How's the team doing without me?" Noah asked.

"Eh, we're killing them," Josh replied. "We beat Central by 20 points last week."

Noah thought for a moment. If he could get Josh

to answer enough questions, he might learn something he could use, or at least find proof that his memories were not wrong. "What about the track team?"

Josh shrugged. "Season's over."

"I know, but how did it go?"

"Not sure. I never did see why you were so interested in all that running." Josh got up from the chair and paced around the small room. He moved his hand up and down as if he were dribbling a basketball. "If I'm going to run all over the place, I'm going to get some points scored."

"Don't lie to me," said Noah. "The only reason you ever played basketball was so you could be close to the cheerleaders."

Josh turned and gave a broad smile. "It does keep them handy. Without you to slow me down, I've gone through the ranks like a shark through water."

Noah couldn't help but smile back. "What about Caroline?"

"What?" Josh clamped his hand to his heart. "You're accusing me of violating my sacred trust, of betraying my dearest friend, of trying to move in on the girlfriend of a guy in a *coma?* I am deeply offended."

Noah laughed. "So she turned you down cold, huh?"

Josh held up three fingers. "Three times. Can you believe it?" He sighed heavily. "There is no accounting for taste."

For the second time, Noah felt doubt edging into his thoughts. This *was* the Josh he had known. It seemed impossible that everything around him could be a lie and Josh could be so real. "Is Coach Rocklin still there?"

"Rocklin?" Josh looked puzzled. "Who's Rocklin?"

"The girl's track coach."

"Oh, the blond. Yeah, I think so." He thumped back into the chair and looked at Noah. "What's all this interest in the track team? You planning on being a marathon man?"

"There's a girl on the team I like," said Noah.

Josh leaned toward the bed. "Oh, yeah? You mean Caroline's been holding out on me for nothing? Give. Who is this fast beauty?"

"The new girl," said Noah. "Kathleen Davisidaro."

"Davisidaro?" Josh frowned and looked up at the ceiling. "Kathleen Davisidaro." He shrugged. "Rings no bells with me. When did she start at school?"

"October. About the same time I had my wreck. She calls herself Harley."

"Harley?" Josh held up his hands mimicked twisting the throttle on a motorcycle. "Vroom. Vroom. Sounds like someone I ought to know."

"Maybe you've seen her around school," Noah suggested. "Kind of tall. Dark hair. Very pretty?"

Josh pursed his lips. "If there was anyone like that around school, I would have *definitely* noticed."

Noah frowned. Josh's story matched his mother's. He ran his mind over the other things that had happened over the last few weeks. There had to be something he could use to prove to himself that his memories were right.

"So," said Josh. "You going to play basketball down in Florida?"

"Florida? What do you mean?"

"Didn't your parents talk to you?" asked Josh.

"About what?"

Josh frowned. "Maybe I shouldn't have said anything."

"But you did," said Noah. "So you might as well spill the rest."

"Well, I'm not sure about this, you understand," Josh replied, "but from what I hear, you're dad's planning on moving to Florida."

Noah digested the news for a moment. His father had talked about moving before, but he had always backed out. In the November of Noah's memories, his parents had never even brought up the idea. But in this November—in the November of car wrecks and hospital rooms—his parents had decided to move. It took him only a moment to think of what would have tipped the scales. *If they move, they can keep me from checking up on my real past.*

Someone was behind this false world. Whoever it was, they had provided a fake hospital, and a fake Josh, and Noah's parents. But they couldn't replace the whole town of Stone Harbor. If Noah went home again, there would be plenty of people he could talk to about what had happened over the last month. There were the other students at school. If there had been a car wreck, they would all know about it. If there *hadn't* been a car wreck, they would know that too.

"Florida," he said slowly. "I guess it'll be a lot warmer down there."

"Yeah," said Josh. "Babes in bikinis all year long." He stretched his hands above his head and arched his back. "Maybe I ought to go with you. You know, help you settle in."

Noah slumped down in his bed.

Josh quickly jumped to his feet. "You feeling okay?"

"Yeah," Noah said softly. "I'm all right. I'm just feeling kind of tired."

"You want me to get a Doctor?"

"No. Just a little more sleep is all I need."

Josh nodded. "Okay. But you better get up quick. Otherwise, we might not get that chance for one-on-one." He gave Noah another thump on the arm and strolled out of the room.

Noah waited until Josh was gone, then slowly swung his legs over to the side of the bed. He had been careful to tell the Doctor and his parents that his legs were still frozen, but the truth was that he had been recovering rapidly. Carefully, he slid off the bed and pressed his weight against the floor.

His knees wobbled, and for a terrifying second he thought he was going to fall. He leaned against the bed and took a shuffling step. Then he moved his arms a little further along and took another step. Three steps took him to the end of the bed. He stared across the gulf between the bed and the wall like it was the Grand Canyon.

Noah felt like a toddler taking his first step. He took a deep breath and launched out. His feet slipped, his knees shook, and his arms flailed through the air, but he did not fall. He thumped up against the wall and pressed his face to the blue paint, his heart beating rapidly. With his hands on the wall, Noah slid to the door and looked out.

The hospital hallway looked completely normal. Noah wasn't sure exactly what he had expected—maybe something like a movie set, with stagehands standing behind false walls and lights hanging down to illuminate the scene. All he saw was a long hallway with a tiled white floor and a series of wooden doors marked with small numbers. In the distance, a PA system summoned a Doctor to the emergency room.

Noah moved away from the door and shuffled toward the window. He put a finger between the metal slats of the venetian blind and pulled them open. Outside, the trees were bare, but the sky was blue. Cars moved along the street, and a boy on a bike peddled by, a red scarf flying out behind him.

Normal. It was all painfully normal.

Frustrated, Noah made his way back to the bed and lay down. Josh had skillfully avoided any area of conversation where Noah might find a problem. His parents were planning to move him to Florida. Noah bet that the move would happen soon, before he got a chance to talk to anyone else from Stone Harbor. If he was going to find proof that he wasn't crazy, he had to find it right where he was.

He closed his eyes and searched again for the thread that lead away from his body. He needed to reach the nexus, and to move beyond it to Harley. Noah had learned to leave his body and travel to the nexus of dreams even before Umbra had removed the walls from his abilities. If he could reach the nexus again, it would be a first step to regaining everything he had lost.

But after long moments of concentration, Noah groaned and opened his eyes. All he found in his mind was a strange *slickness*, like a prison of glass.

Noah's gaze fell on the chart at the end of the bed.

He was willing to bet that it was carefully filled out, and matched every detail of the story he had been told, but it didn't hurt to check. He twisted around in the bed and snatched the chart. Just as he had thought, the charts contained almost two months worth of notes. There were descriptions of Noah's original injuries "Cranial Frac. R.F. See film." and notes on his daily condition and medication.

He raised his hand to his head and felt through his hair. He couldn't find any wound, or bump, but then it had been two months from the date of the wreck. Even if he really had been injured, there had been plenty of time to heal.

Noah froze. There had been plenty of time for his head to heal from the injury of the make-believe wreck. But in his memories, he had received another injury. Falling rocks had hit him on the chest. Unless he really had been asleep for weeks, those injuries had to still be there.

He reached down to the large buttons on his pajamas and pulled them open. His heart sank. The skin of his chest was smooth and unmarked. There was no sign of the injuries he remembered.

Because they never happened, he thought. You were looking for proof, now you have it. All your memories of Harley are nothing more than dreams.

"No, it was real," he said, his voice growing louder with every word. "It is real!"

He reached down to his chest and ran his fingers over his skin. He touched the place where the stone had struck him and pressed hard.

A bolt of pain shot though Noah's body. For a

moment, he saw a cloud of ugly yellow and purple bruises on his chest.

It wasn't only his skin that changed. The light around him grew dim, and the furniture of the room became as transparent as colored glass. Through them and beyond them Noah could see a vast place of darkness and fear. He took his hand away from his broken rib, and the hospital room instantly returned to normal.

Noah grinned at the empty room. "I've got you," he whispered. "I've found the key."

His last shadows of doubt were gone. The people that had him were good, almost impossibly good, but they would never fool him again. He knew what was real and what was illusion.

He flexed his legs. They were still stiff and weak, but they were better every time he tried. It wasn't quite time for his escape, but that time was coming soon. Very soon.

"Are you sure this is a good idea?" asked Harley. She looked into the dark elevator shaft on the twelfth floor of Water Tower Place. She had climbed down it once, but what she was preparing to do now seemed a lot more frightening.

Kenyon adjusted a strap around her shoulders. "It'll work," he said. "Trust me."

Harley turned and looked into his dark eyes. *"Trust me?* Is that the best you can do?"

"It'll have to do," said Kenyon. He tugged on a cord and stepped back from Harley. "You're all set."

"I hope so." Harley turned her head and looked into the open elevator shaft behind her. "I can't believe I agreed to this."

The elevator in the center of the lobby chimed and the door slid open. Dee and Scott stepped out carrying a wire mesh cage between them. In the center of the cage was the golden orb.

"Are you sure that thing will keep Unit 17 from finding the orb?" asked Harley. To her, the cage looked like something for keeping a rabbit.

Scott set the cage on the floor in front of Harley. "It should work as long as the current flows," he said. "Unless they're using something that's outside the normal range of radiation."

"And if they are?"

"Then who knows? The cage might block it, do

nothing, or even amplify it. Without knowing what to look for there's no way to tell."

Harley looked down at the metal ball. "How comforting."

Kenyon clapped his hands sharply. "All right," he said. "Everything is in place up here. We need to move down to two."

Scott and Dee headed back into the elevator. Kenyon started to follow, but Harley reached out and grabbed him by the arm. "Shouldn't we test this gear first?"

Kenyon looked at her, and then the elevator shaft. "Are you certain you want to do this twice?"

"I don't even want to do it once!" Harley cried.

Kenyon stepped past her and looked into the elevator shaft. "I don't think testing is a good idea."

"Why not?"

"Because you're wearing a minimal rig," said Kenyon. "It would be best not to subject it to repeated shocks."

Harley felt as if she had swallowed a whole forest full of butterflies. "Please explain to me why this is a good thing."

"Don't worry," said Kenyon. He reached down, removed the orb from its cage, and handed it to Harley. "Be ready," he said. "There's no way to know how long this will take."

He stepped into the elevator, and the doors slid shut. Harley was alone with her worries and the golden sphere. She walked as far as she could from the elevator and looked around, but the cord at her back kept her from going too far. The sphere in her hands was warm, and she could feel its faint, deep humming against her palms. "Call them quick," she whispered to the metal ball. "I'm too nervous to wait here all afternoon."

Ten minutes passed, then fifteen. Harley leaned back against the bare metal wall beside the elevator shaft and closed her eyes. She could hear the faint sound of traffic from the street twelve floors below. A faint tick came from somewhere in the building. It startled her at first, and she tensed, but nothing happened. A few minutes later, the sound came again, and once more a few minutes after that. Harley relaxed. Construction had stopped on Water Tower Place, but the electricity in the building was still on. The sound was probably nothing more than a switch in the heating system or the air ducts.

Harley was half asleep when the door to the stairwell flew open. Braddock's approach was anything but subtle this time. He stormed across the concrete floor at a trot, three soldiers at his side. They approached Harley with their guns drawn.

Harley moved to stand in front of the open elevator shaft. She was careful to keep facing them, hiding her back and the cord until the last possible second. Her heart pounded as she watched the men slow and form a semicircle around her. The plan that had sounded so good back at the penthouse suddenly sounded very, *very* foolish.

Commander Braddock stopped ten feet in front of Harley. He held one of the strange guns the men at the hospital had used—a sliver gun, the heavy man had called it. The narrow opening at the front of the gun was small, but it presented a certain deadliness that had nothing to do with size.

"Ms. Davisidaro," said Braddock. He looked her up and down. "I assume you expected we would find you here."

"Yes," said Harley. She was embarrassed to hear a quiver of nervousness in her voice.

"Then you've decided to come with us willingly?"

"Not quite." Harley licked her dry lips and cleared her throat. "I want Noah and my father," she said. "When you turn them both over to me, and promise never to bother us again, I'll hand over the sphere."

Braddock gave a bitter laugh. "Is that your best offer?"

"No," replied Harley. "Those are my demands."

"You're in no position to make demands," sneered Braddock. "I don't have your father. I don't have your friend. What I do have is *you.*" He nodded to the soldiers. "Take her." The men holstered their weapons and started toward Harley.

"Wait!" She took a step back. The heels over her tennis shoes hung over the void.

"That will do you no good," said Braddock. "We've posted a man by your little sliding board. There's no escaping this time."

"We'll see about that," Harley replied.

Braddock made growling sound deep in his throat. "I'm tired of dealing with you, Ms. Davisidaro. You may be useful to us, but it is the orb we really need. Give it to me this instant, or I will shoot you and take it from your dead fingers."

"You want it? Then come and get it!" Harley jumped back from the lip of the shaft.

For a moment, she seemed to hang in the air. She

saw Braddock raising his weapon, and the soldiers lunging toward her. Then gravity remembered her, and she hurtled toward the ground. She saw the number 11 stenciled on the concrete wall as she passed the next floor. Beyond that, it was only a dark and terrifying blur.

This particular part of the plan had been Scott's idea. Harley heard his words playing in her head as the ground rushed up to smash her. "Bungee jumping's great," he had said. "I've done it a hundred times. You'll love it."

As she rocketed past the tenth floor, and the ninth, and eight, and seventh, Harley thought that Scott had to be the craziest person she had ever met. Anyone that did this *once* was nuts.

As the floors whipped past, Harley felt a growing sense of certainty. She was going to die. The cord attached to her back was no thicker than her little finger. It couldn't possibly stop this awful fall. She would hit the ground and be nothing but a bloody smear in the bottom of the elevator shaft. Or the cord would hold, but it would stop her so suddenly that her back would snap in half like a stale pretzel. Either way, she was dead.

Half a second later, the cord grew taut. Harley swung down past the third floor, and the second. Her speed dropped quickly, but she was within ten feet of the ground before she was pulled back into the air.

Two pairs of arms reached out from the second floor and grabbed her as she passed. Together, Kenyon and Scott pulled Harley from the shaft and unbuckled her harness.

"How was the ride?" asked Scott. "Pretty cool, eh?"

Harley could not reply at first. Her heart had taken a vacation from her chest and was beating at the back of her throat. She wanted to fall down on the hard floor and hug the concrete. Only after two deep, ragged breaths did she manage to squeak out a reply. "That was awful!"

Scott frowned. "Sorry," he said. "Maybe next time you can try jumping someplace nicer."

"Never again," Harley gasped. "I think I'd rather be shot."

Kenyon leaned past her and looked up the shaft. "I believe that can be easily arranged. If we don't get into our places, Unit 17 will see that you never make another jump."

Kenyon and Scott moved quickly to take their prearranged spots. Harley stepped into the center of a small hallway and waited.

This time, the wait was very short. Unit 17 soldiers came out of the stairwell at a hard run. "Halt there!" called one of the first men through the door. "Or we'll shoot!"

"I'm not going anyplace," said Harley. She raised her hands and the gold orb, above her head. "Come and get me."

The soldiers came forward quickly, their eyes focused only on Harley. Commander Braddock led the pack, a snarl on his lips and fire in his gray eyes. They were within ten feet when the plasterboard walls at their side suddenly tumbled down on them. An eight-foot-tall white sheet cracked down on Braddock's head. Plaster dust showered the blue shoulders of his uniform, and the commander's knees buckled. The soldier behind him stumbled and fell against his leader. In a moment, the Unit 17 men were a pile of squirming arms.

Before the men could rise, Dee, Scott, and Kenyon stepped out from behind the fallen walls. In their hands they held the bulky forms of the Taser pistols.

"Now!" shouted Kenyon.

All three of them fired together. The Tasers spat metal spikes and a stream of cable into the men. As the spikes struck home in flesh, blue sparks played over the fallen soldiers and Braddock. The Taser guns gave out a high pitched whine. The soldiers' bodies twisted and twitched like catfish on a hot skillet. Harley smelled the sharp bite of ozone mingled with the awful, sickening smell of singed hair.

"That's enough," said Kenyon. "Shut them off."

Harley walked over to join the others. She looked down at the heap of unconscious soldiers in amazement. "It worked."

"Of course it did," said Kenyon. "I planned it." He shoved the Taser into an oversized holster on his belt and knelt down beside the men. "Go bring the vehicle up to the door," he ordered. "And put the orb back in its cage so they can't follow us. We'll be out in a second."

Scott took the orb from Harley, then he and Dee hurried to get the van.

Harley joined Kenyon beside the fallen soldiers. Commander Braddock's face was just visible at the edge of the pile. "Do you think we can get him out?"

Instead of answering, Kenyon grabbed the Unit 17 commander by the arms and started pulling. Kenyon's face creased with effort, but after a moment, Braddock began to come free of the pile. As he was pulled away from the others, Braddock opened his eyes and groaned.

"Shoot them," he mumbled. "Shoot them all."

"You missed your chance for that," said Kenyon. He released Braddock's arms and let the stocky man fall to the ground. Braddock gave a faint groan, then closed his eyes again.

"Okay," said Harley. "You grab the feet, and I'll grab the arms."

"That won't be necessary," said Kenyon. He pulled out his Taser and crouched beside Braddock. "Wake up!" he shouted at the stunned commander. "I want you to see this!"

Harley took a step toward Kenyon. "What are you doing? This isn't part of the plan."

"It's part of *my* plan." Kenyon put the point of the Taser against Braddock's forehead and leaned down until his face was only inches from the Unit 17 leader's. "Your group killed my parents," he growled. "I don't know if you're the big dog, or only one of the rats, but it's time somebody paid."

"Wait!" Harley dived forward and shoved Kenyon's arm away. The Taser fired its metal bolt against the floor with a loud clank, sending a shower of sparks skittering over the concrete. "Are you nuts?" Harley shouted at Kenyon. "Exactly *what* are you trying to do?"

"Kill him," Kenyon replied with icy calm. He zipped the cord back into the Taser and returned his aim to Braddock. "This is supposed to be a nonlethal weapon, but I think ten thousand volts sent straight to his skull ought to do the trick. Don't you?"

Harley stepped between Braddock and Kenyon. "We're not supposed to kill him. We're going to take him prisoner, remember?"

"I changed my mind." Kenyon finished reloading the Taser and raised it again. "Now move out of the way."

"Or what?" Harley crossed over arms over her chest and glared at Kenyon. "Are you going to shoot me too? Your parents are dead, and I'm sorry about that. But my dad is still alive. And with Braddock dead, we may lose our only way of finding him."

For a moment, Kenyon stood with his weapon pointing at Harley and the same expression of icy calm on his face. Then his hand began to tremble. "Move out of the way," he said again, but instead of his usual commanding tone, his voice sounded confused and weak.

"No," said Harley.

"Move," whispered Kenyon. He stood for a moment longer, then dropped the Taser. The heavy weapon thumped to the gray concrete, and the plastic door of a battery cover bounced away. A shudder ran through Kenyon from top to bottom, and he let out a deep moan. He turned away and stood with his back to Harley.

Harley bit her lip. She had known almost since she met Kenyon that Unit 17 had killed his parents. It gave them a common enemy. But Kenyon always seemed so tough. He never admitted to any weakness. Harley had seen how angry he could be, but until that moment, she hadn't even guessed at the pain he felt over his parent's death.

"Kenyon," she said softly. "I'm sorry."

"It's not your fault." Kenyon drew in a ragged breath. When he turned back again, his usual hard expression was in place. "All right. Let's get this jerk out to the van."

Commander Braddock moaned and groaned, and thrashed weakly as they half carried, half dragged him out to the van. Once there, they slid a black cloth sack over his head and bound his hands behind his back with strapping tape. Thirty minutes later, they had Braddock back at the penthouse.

By the time they finished taping him to a chair, Braddock had recovered from his Taser shot. "I don't know what you expect to accomplish by this," he said as Harley wound yard after yard of tape binding his ankle to one of the chair legs. "Holding me does nothing but sign your death warrant."

"Shut up," snapped Kenyon. "Or I'll put some of this tape over your mouth."

Commander Braddock laughed. "Wouldn't that defeat the purpose?" he asked. "Didn't you bring me here to talk?"

Harley wound a last length of tape around Braddock's legs, then stood up. Dee was throwing things around in one bedroom, cleaning out a place to hold Braddock. Scott was tuned into his handmade radios, monitoring Unit 17's response to Braddock's capture. Kenyon stood beside the commander, methodically wrapping enough tape around Braddock's body to pin down an elephant. Against the elegant backdrop of the penthouse, it all looked impossibly bizarre.

Finally, Kenyon decided Braddock was secure. "There. He's not going anywhere."

"Oh, I'm going somewhere," the commander

said from behind his cloth mask. "I'll walk out of here whenever I'm ready."

"Give me back my father and Noah," Harley said, "and we'll let you go."

"Do you think I have them in my pocket, Ms. Davisidaro?" asked Braddock.

Harley dragged a chair over to sit a few feet in front of Braddock, the sat down. "I don't think they're in your pocket," she said, "but I think you have them. And you're going to stay right here until you decide to let them go."

"Then we'll both be here a very long time," Braddock replied.

Kenyon walked around the commander like a lion circling its prey. "We don't have to just sit here," he said.

"What do you mean?" Harley asked.

"Only that we might speed things along." Kenyon walked over to the fireplace and picked up a poker. He held the metal rod up for a moment, examining it, then thrust the point into the flames. "For example, if we heat this until it's nice and red, then apply it to a few tender spots, he may get very talkative very quickly."

"Who are you?" Braddock asked. Despite the sack over his head and the tape that bound him hand and foot, Braddock's voice was still that of a man who expected others to obey his orders. "Answer me, boy. What makes you think you can get away with touching me?"

"Your group killed my parents," said Kenyon. "I'll do whatever I want to you."

"A great number of people have died to serve the cause," Braddock replied. "If you want to identify yourself, you'll have to give me a better clue than that."

Kenyon growled low in his throat. He pulled out the poker and examined the smoking tip. "I believe I'll start with the hands," he said. "And then maybe the eyes."

A sick feeling settled in Harley's stomach. She wasn't sure if Kenyon was serious or not. She hated Braddock for his part in taking away her father, and the way he had tortured her when he had the chance, but she wasn't ready to start returning that torture.

"Do whatever you like," said Braddock. "But it won't get you what you want."

"Where is my father?" Harley demanded.

"That's difficult to explain," Braddock answered, and to Harley's surprise he continued. "He developed a new transportation technique, a very special technique, but in our experiments, he was lost."

"Lost where?"

"Everywhere and nowhere," Braddock replied.

"You see?" said Kenyon. "He's not going to tell you anything unless we ask in a way that men like him can understand." He walked over to the commander and held the glowing poker close to his face. "Where is Harley's father?"

"As I said, he is lost. If Ms. Davisidaro will cooperate, we may be able to retrieve him."

"Where is Noah?"

"On that point," said Braddock, "I can be of no assistance. I have no idea where this Noah person may be."

"But I do," said a voice from across the room.

Harley turned to see Scott sitting beside his radios. "What did you say?" she asked.

Scott's usual grin had grown into a full-fledged smile. "I think I found Noah," he said.

Noah's mother came in at sunset, with a big smile on her face and a hefty chocolate cake in her hands. "Are you ready for a break from this hospital food?"

Noah nodded. "But I thought you didn't approve of sweets. You haven't fixed anything like that in years."

"This is a special occasion," his mother replied. "You don't get your only son back from a coma every day. Besides, I thought since you slept through Thanksgiving, you might appreciate a chance to sample some of the goodies you missed."

The smell of the cake made Noah feel more than a little ill. It wasn't that he didn't like chocolate, but he had had his fill of lies and deceptions. "How nice," he said.

His sarcastic tone made his mother pause. The fragile smile on her face drooped. She put the cake down on the table at his bedside and took her place in the chair. "What's wrong, Noah? Are you feeling well?"

"I'm feeling fine," said Noah. "I'm feeling great, in fact." That was true enough when it came to his physical feelings. His legs were getting stronger by the minute and the rest of his body already felt fine.

But when it came to emotions, Noah didn't know how to feel. He looked at the woman in the chair and felt swamped by a mixture of betrayal and confusion. He couldn't believe that his own parents were no more than agents of a secret organization. That could mean his whole life was nothing but a seventeen-year-long science experiment. Legion had bred him like a show dog and planted him with a family where he could be watched over. Everything in his life was built on a stack of lies so deep he no longer knew where to look to find the truth.

One thing Noah was sure of—he was very tired of this particular lie. "I wasn't here for Thanksgiving," he said.

"Of course you weren't," his mother replied. "You were in that awful coma."

Noah shook his head. "No. I was kidnapped by Umbra. When Thanksgiving came, I was in a cell in their headquarters."

"Is this more of that awful dream?" She frowned. "I thought you'd gotten past that, Noah."

"It wasn't a dream."

The look of concern on his mother's face was so real Noah almost believed she really cared. "Noah, maybe it's time we called in professional help. I talked to Dr. Ripley about your dreams. He says there's a very good psychiatrist right here in this—"

"Don't talk to me about a psychiatrist!" Noah shouted with a force that surprised even him. "I'm not crazy."

"No, of course not," his mother said patiently. "But when you've been through something as awful as this wreck, you've got to expect that there will be some problems. We'll get through this together, Noah. I know you'll be just fine."

Noah pressed his hands to the side of his head.

"Stop it!" he cried. "Don't you realize I'm onto you? I know about Doctor Ripley, and the aliens. I know this whole place is a lie."

His mother's face crumpled. "We only want you to get well."

"No. More. Lies," Noah barked, biting off each word between his clenched teeth. He took his right hand and viciously slammed it against his injured chest.

The bolt of pain that went through his body was amazing. Noah's back arched and his neck snapped back from the sheer force of the agony. Around him, the hospital dissolved like a chalk painting in the rain. The soft bed was once again a cold slab of bare metal. Noah's soft pajamas became the same tattered clothes he had been wearing when he was taken by Umbra weeks before.

But this time there was another change. The woman by his bed was no longer his mother. In her place was a considerably younger woman with thin, sharp features and pale blue eyes. It was the face of a stranger. Relief washed over Noah—his parents were not part of this trap after all. They were only part of the illusion.

"Who are you?" Noah gasped. "You're not my mom."

"Noah?" cried the woman. "How can you say that?"

"Ditch it, lady." Noah sat up and swiveled around to face her. "I can see you. I know you're not my mother."

For the first time, the woman hesitated. "I don't know what you're talking about."

"You're about thirty years old. You've got brown hair

and blue eyes," said Noah. "You're *not* my mother."

The stranger's eyes went wide. "How did . . . I mean, what are you talking about?"

"I'm talking about an end to the lies," said Noah. "I can see everything." He raised his voice to a shout. "Do you hear me? I see it all! You can't lie to me anymore!"

Dr. Ripley emerged from the shadows. "Bravo, Mr. Templer," he said. "Once again, you exceed all expectations."

The strange woman who had acted the role of Noah's mother stood up quickly. "I didn't do anything, Doctor. I didn't tell him." There was fear in her voice, as if she expected punishment.

"Of course you didn't, Stephanie." Ripley replied. "Please leave us alone now."

The woman nodded and walked away into the darkness.

Doctor Ripley put his hands in his pockets and looked at Noah with an unreadable expression. "Do you know where you are?"

The dark place, Noah wanted to say. It was the place of terror which had haunted his dreams. He pushed those fears away and tried to keep his voice as calm as Ripley's. "This is Legion."

"Wrong. Legion is not a place, Mr. Templer." Ripley began to pace slowly back and forth. "Legion is a group of dedicated people who have worked over a space of centuries."

"People like you," said Noah.

Ripley paused and looked toward Noah. "Yes, and like you."

Noah shook his head. "I'm not part of your club."

"Oh, but you are." Ripley gestured at the room around them. "I asked you if you knew what this place is, but it's obvious that you do not."

"This is where I've been tortured," said Noah.

Dr. Ripley shook his head. "This is where you were born."

The words sent a chill through Noah. "I was born in Creek County Hospital."

"No, you were born here." Dr. Ripley came closer and his voice grew more intense. "Think of it, Noah. All those other people in the world are no more than accidents. Their parents sat together in some high-school class, or maybe they met on a job—it's all co-incidence." He reached out and put a hand on Noah's shoulder. "But we left nothing to chance when we created you. Every gene, every nucleotide, is just as we wanted it."

A deep sense of horror washed over Noah. "No," he said. "That's another lie."

"You know it's not," said Ripley.

Noah wanted to protest again, but he knew that this time the Doctor was hiding nothing. This was the awful truth behind the dark room that had terrified him—his own origins. Suddenly Noah wished he had stuck with the lies. "I'm nothing but an experiment."

"No, you are a *triumph*. The structure of your mind alone is the result of five centuries of work."

"I'm a lab rat," Noah moaned.

"You are the next stage in evolution! With a mind like yours, anything is possible." Ripley took his hand from Noah's shoulder and moved a few steps away. "Well, Mr. Templer. Now that you know the truth, what do you think?"

Noah's mind was swirling with emotions he couldn't even name, but there were still a few things he could be sure of. "I think you and your whole organization are a bunch of psychos," he spat out. "And I want nothing to do with you or your next step in evolution crap."

"You'll be leaving very soon." Ripley clapped his hands together and then swept them through the air like a magician performing sleight of hand. When his hands stopped, they held a gleaming metallic spike. It was more than a foot long, and wickedly sharp. The base was as thick as Noah's thumb, but it tapered quickly to a point that glittered in the hard overhead light.

Looking at the spike brought a fear which pushed all other emotions aside. "What are you going to do with that?" Noah asked.

Dr. Ripley raised his left hand and pointed into the shadows. Immediately Noah heard a deep throbbing hum.

Paralysis dropped over Noah. This was not the gentle paralysis he had worked to overcome in the hospital room. This was the all-enclosing stillness that he had experienced in his dark dreams. He fell back against the metal slab, unable to move his limbs or even blink.

He knew now that none of his dark visions had been dreams. The images that had haunted him were not nightmares, but tangled memories of the times Legion had brought him to this place to check on their pet freak.

From the shadows, the aliens gathered.

Noah saw eight of them, small and white, with bloated heads and huge flat, black eyes. They rushed forward with a soft, dry rustling sound.

Ripley drew near. "I'm sure you have wondered about these figures that surround you," he said. "It will harm nothing now for you to know the truth." He raised his left hand again, and a row of eight lights appeared in the darkness.

Beneath each light was what looked at first like a large aquarium. But these aquariums did not hold fish. Locked within cases of milky translucent fluid were eight human bodies. The bodies were a mixture of male and female, and different races. But from what Noah could see, all of them appeared to be elderly. Thin white hair floated around wrinkled faces. Thin, wasted limbs bumped softly against the glass walls. Toothless mouths gaped open and gnarled hands were tightened into knobby fists. Pale, lifeless eyes stared sightlessly outward through the glass.

"These are the greatest surviving Legion members of centuries past," announced Ripley. He strolled along the row of floating bodies. "They have mastered mental abilities undreamed of by those outside of Legion. Our advances in science had allowed them to survive long past the time when death would have normally claimed them." He turned and gestured toward the circle of white figures. "And their own great mental powers have allowed them to divorce their *Kah-em* from their decaying flesh."

The white faces circled around Noah, blank eyes looking down. For so long, he had thought they were aliens. Once again, the truth seemed even worse than the lies. Alien life-forms were not prodding and poking about his mind and body. They were the disembodied souls of men and women who should have died long ago.

Noah struggled to move, but he could manage not even a twitch. Unable to use his body, he reached out with his mind. He searched down inside himself and tried to grip the powers that had come so easily before Legion had put up their new barriers. It was like trying to claw through a sheet of steel.

One of the white figures made a crackling, hissing sound.

"Is he?" Dr. Ripley walked back to the table and leaned over Noah. "I'm informed you're trying to exercise the abilities which we have engineered into your mind."

Anger flared in Noah. He was not a lab rat! He concentrated on the image of gleaming walls that cut him off from his powers. Then he gathered his furious thoughts into a ball and hurled them at that wall.

The white form at his side made a noise like crumpling paper.

"You may as well stop," advised Dr. Ripley. "The new blocks we placed in your mind are the strongest we've ever created. You'll never get past them." He raised the metal spike and sighted down its length. "I know you must be upset, Noah. Don't worry. In a moment, you won't feel a thing."

Noah reached deeper, going beyond the surface of his mind. He could still see a spark there—a glimmer of light not covered over by Ripley's walls. Noah gathered that light and threw it against the barriers. It splashed away without penetrating the blocks, but it left behind a small dent.

Ripley lowered the point of the gleaming probe until it was only inches from Noah's face. "Your emotions have interfered with the course of our work for too long. Fear and confusion, anger and love—these are all needless wastes of mental activity."

Noah reached down and hurled his thoughts again. The dent in the barriers grew deeper.

"If you had only accepted the lovely little fiction we had concocted for you," said Ripley. "You could be lying on a beach in Florida. Instead we'll have to take other actions."

Like a man hammering his way into a mountain, Noah threw out his energy again and again. The dent grew deeper and wider, but the walls held.

"Your mind is far too valuable to be used by such a simple, emotional boy." Ripley rolled the probe between his fingers and moved it slowly forward. "You're merely a vessel. Once your mind is fully prepared, one of these *Kah-em* gathered around you will gain control of your mind and body." All of the white figures rustled like trees in a winter wind.

On the outside, Noah lay frozen, his eyes fixed on the needle-sharp point of the approaching probe. Inside, he desperately pounded at the mental walls. Cracks spread as the barriers began to loosen. But it was happening too slowly. Far too slowly.

The point of the probe paused a fraction of an inch from Noah's left eye. "We had hoped to deliver your mind completely intact. However, it appears that a slight modification is in order. With this instrument, I will administer a highly modified frontal lobotomy. Hate, anger, fear, love, and caring—all those things will be only memories."

Noah reached deeper. He went far beyond his mind and down into his heart and his guts. He found a power there that had nothing to do with the mind. It was all raw, red fury and frustration generated by a lifetime of lies. From the base of his spine he gathered a surge of power and channeled it up like a geyser. It stuck Legion's walls and threw them aside like a hurricane striking a barrier of straw.

"No!" shouted Noah. His left hand whipped up and snatched the probe away from Ripley. His right hand curled into a fist and struck the Doctor squarely in the mouth.

Ripley fell back with blood dripping from his shredded lips. "It's not possible!" he cried. Each word came out in a spray of crimson droplets.

Noah swung his legs off the side of the table and stood. The white figures of the disembodied leaders gave way before him sighing and swaying like trees in a storm.

"Anything's possible with a mind like mine," said Noah. "You said so yourself. Now, show me the way out of this place."

Ripley's face contorted in rage. "There is no way out, Mr. Templer. Not for you." The Doctor raised his left hand again, and red lights appeared in the darkness. A warning buzzer began to shriek.

Noah ran toward the Doctor and slashed out with

the metal spike. The point tore through Ripley's palm, leaving a deep dent in the meat of his hand. The Doctor gasped and clutched his injured hand against his chest. Deep red stains spread across the front of his white coat.

"Tell me where I get out," Noah demanded, "or the next time I'll put it right through your shriveled, useless heart."

Ripley's chin quivered, but he shook his head. "Kill me if you want. The great work of the cause will go on!"

Noah raised the probe, then turned away. Instead of slashing at Ripley, he brought the probe down against the nearest of the human aquariums. The first blow cracked the glass, the second broke it open like a rotten pumpkin. A flood of pale fluid rushed around Noah's legs. With it came the body of an old man. The shriveled thing spilled out onto the floor and lay there as boneless and unmoving as a beached jellyfish. Beside Noah, one of the white figures flickered and disappeared.

"Stop!" demanded Ripley. "That man's mind held the knowledge of centuries!"

Noah raised the probe over the next glass coffin. "If you want to save these pickled *things*, you better show me the way out of here. Now!"

Ripley raised a shaking hand and pointed into the gloom. "That way," he said. "And may you come to the end you deserve."

"Same to you," Noah replied. As he turned to leave, one of the white forms blocked his way. Noah jabbed at it with the probe, but it was like stabbing

Jell-O. The probe left no mark in the glowing form. Disgusted, Noah kicked out and sent the thing flying aside. The brief contact with the creature left his foot tingling.

Noah charged past, moving as fast as he could on legs that were still stiff. The mad Doctor and his seven dwarfish monstrosities vanished behind him in the darkness. As he stumbled on in the direction Ripley had indicated, Noah heard other footsteps approaching and voices raised in anger.

"That way!" Noah heard Ripley cry. "He went that way!"

Noah hurried on, hoping to catch sight of a doorway or even a wall, but he saw nothing. The blackness seemed impenetrable in all directions. It was worse than Umbra's cave. At least in the caves there had been a stream to follow and walls close on either hand. In Legion's headquarters there seemed to be nothing but nothing.

And then he was out. He didn't press through a door, or go through any opening that he could see. On one step he was running through the endless darkness. On the next he fell into a wide corridor with bare lightbulbs dangling from the ceiling on cords and dozens of pipes running along the walls.

Noah turned and looked behind him. The wall looked like solid brick. He ran his hands over the rough surface and found no opening. After a moment, he decided it didn't matter how he got out. He was out, and that's what was important.

He turned, and had gone no more than a dozen yards down the corridor when he heard a soft popping sound behind him. Noah looked over his shoulder and saw a man in a white lab coat standing in the hallway. The popping sound came again, and another man appeared. The two men ran toward Noah.

Noah turned around and did his best to stay ahead. He reached a branch in the corridor and turned right, at another branch he turned left. The corridor grew wider, and the lighting was brighter. Noah saw another man ahead and almost stopped, but this man looked different. He was dressed in a brown suit and pushed a metal cart stacked with old leather-bound books. Instead of running away from the man, Noah dashed toward him.

"Where am I?" Noah asked.

The man pushing the cart looked up. Fear showed on his face as he looked at Noah. "You . . . you're between the Office of Engraving and the, the . . . the Library of Congress," he stuttered.

"Library of Congress?" Noah recognized the name. He was still in Washington. "Which way to the library?"

The man pointed down the corridor. "It's that way. But you look like you ought to be seeing a Doctor."

"No thanks," said Noah. "I saw one already." The sound of approaching steps told Noah it was time to leave. He ran past the man and charged on down the hallway. Fifty feet ahead, he could see where the corridor opened into a large room.

He heard a sharp clank from his right, and something fast went whining away down the hall. Noah glanced back and saw that the two men in white were closing in on him. He turned around to put on a final burst of speed.

Noah felt a sudden sharp pain in his leg. He stumbled a step, came close to falling, then struggled on.

He entered a large room and passed two very startled library workers. He turned a corner and entered a room filled with row after row of books. At the far side, at least two hundred feet away, was a glowing sign marked with the wonder word Exit. Noah put his head down and took two strides toward the sign when his left leg suddenly became as weak and useless as a wet noodle.

Noah fell facedown and went skidding across the dusty floor. His shoulder banged painfully against a shelf, and he came to a stop facing a sign with the strange label PR9619. He rolled over and saw a slender needle jutting from the back of his leg. In a second he had grabbed it and pulled it free, but from the numbness that was now spreading from his left leg into his right, there was no doubt the needle had already delivered its dose of poison.

He could fight the mental paralysis Dr. Ripley had cast over his body, but there was nothing paranormal about the chemicals creeping through Noah's veins. His legs felt as heavy and useless as dead wood.

Footsteps approached. The men from Legion weren't running any more, they were walking slowly, stalking their wounded prey.

Noah put his elbows on the floor and crawled forward like a soldier under enemy fire. A flash of movement caught his attention, and Noah ducked his head. But when the movement came again, Noah saw that it wasn't one of the men in white coats, it was a mechanical device.

"Over here," called a voice from a few rows away. "There's a drop of blood."

He crawled closer to the thing that was moving. It was an immense system of pulleys and chains that never stopped moving—an indoor ski lift. But riding in the trays attached to the chains were not people, but books. They ascended from some deeper basement and traveled up to the world above. Other books were on their way down to storage.

"This way!" shouted one of the men. The voice was much closer, no more than twenty feet away.

Noah pulled himself to the lip of the book lift. He waited a fraction of a second, then he rolled out into space.

He fell a few feet before landing in one of the book trays. The whole lift groaned and shook at the sudden change in weight. For a moment the lift came to a stop. Then, with a series of loud snaps and creaks, the system began to move again.

Noah was six feet above the floor when the men in white emerged from the stacks. They walked past him without seeing, their eyes fixed on the ground as they tried to track him by his spilled blood. A few more seconds, and they were out of sight. Noah rose past one floor, and then another. Yellow light began to glow overhead—not artificial light, but real, honest sunlight.

Noah looked up and smiled as he saw the huge, sunlit reading room of the Library of Congress. Some librarian was about to get a big surprise.

X

TEN

"Are you sure we should have left Dee and Scott alone with Braddock?" Harley asked Kenyon, who was sitting beside her, driving the van.

"No," he replied. "In fact, I think this whole thing is almost certain to be a trap. That's why I brought the orb with us. If Unit 17 shows up at the hotel, I don't want them to get it."

Harley looked at him in surprise. "If you think this is a trap, then why did you come at all?"

"Because you were going."

Once again, Harley wondered if there might be something to Dee's statement that Kenyon liked her. "You mean you didn't want me to get hurt?"

Kenyon nodded. "That's right. You're a very valuable asset to the team. We need your knowledge of the various organizations if we're going to plan an effective strategy."

"An asset," Harley repeated.

"Yes," said Kenyon. "Though you do seem to generate quite a number of difficulties."

Harley fumed silently. Kenyon seemed to think of everything as markers on some big accounting sheet. She was an asset, so she had to be protected. Even his fight with Unit 17 often seemed to be nothing but a debt waiting to be repaid.

But there was emotion underneath Kenyon's cold, rich-kid exterior. Harley had seen some of that emotion

129

when Kenyon had come close to killing Commander Braddock. If he could learn to show something besides his anger at Unit 17, he might be worth knowing.

"This is the place," said Kenyon. He pulled the van over to the side of the road in front of a small brick building with a large brass plaque reading "Colonial History Society."

Harley looked around for any sign of trouble. It was late, and there were few cars on the road. No one else was parked for blocks in either direction, and the sidewalks were empty. "Are you sure this is it?" she asked. "I thought Scott said the radio was buzzing about this place."

"That's what he said." Kenyon opened the glove compartment of the van and pulled out one of the heavy Glock semiautomatic pistols.

"Are you taking that with you?"

"Absolutely," said Kenyon. He pushed open the door and stepped out. Then he leaned back into the van. "And this time, I would strongly advise that you don't stand between me and my target." He slammed the door before Harley could answer.

Harley growled angrily, then shoved the door open on her side and stomped toward the front of the Colonial History building. Kenyon beat her to the door and put his hand over the knob.

"I'll go in first," he said.

"Fine," said Harley. Letting Kenyon lead the way was bound to increase his chance of seeing how well Unit 17's needle guns worked. If he wanted to get shot, Harley wasn't about to stand in his way. "Just make sure you don't shoot Noah."

Kenyon turned the knob. It was unlocked. He pulled open the door slowly. Harley peered over his shoulder, but saw nothing inside but darkness. "All right," he said. "Here we go."

They crept through the entrance hall and out into a round room. Dim light came in through a circle of windows, showing benches against each wall and a raised podium at the center of the room. Harley could see no other doors, and no one present.

"It seems we have a dead end," said Kenyon. He stood up straight and lowered his pistol. "What now?"

Harley shrugged. "You got me." She bent and looked under the benches. "Noah? Are you here?"

"He's not," said a voice from behind them. "But I am."

For a moment, Harley wished she had brought her own gun. She whirled around, expecting to see Unit 17 agents waiting for them.

Instead she saw a single tall figure dressed in a rumpled trench coat and a fedora hat. "Cain?"

"Yes," said the form by the door.

"What are you doing here?" Kenyon demanded.

"I'll be happy to tell you if you'll lower your weapon, Mr. Moor," replied Cain.

Kenyon hesitated a moment, then jammed the pistol into the pocket of his jacket. "Now what are you doing here?"

"I wanted a meeting place," said Cain. "One away from the eyes and ears of others." Lights flared on in the room. "This place seemed as good as any."

Harley blinked and squinted against the sudden brightness. What she saw surprised her. "What happened to you?"

Cain walked toward them. When Harley had first met him, he had claimed to be an agent for the FBI. Since then, she had learned that was a lie. Cain now claimed to work for an organization which was dedicated to policing the other secret societies. Keeping the balance, he had called it.

Whoever Cain worked for, he had gone out of his way to help Harley and Noah on more than one occasion. He had also assisted Kenyon and Scott. Now Cain was the one who looked like he needed help.

The agent stopped at the entrance to the round room. "I've had what might be described as a couple of rough days," he said. From the way he looked, Harley thought Cain must have lived through couple of rough *years* in the space of two days. His skin appeared gray and unhealthy, and there were dark circles around his eyes. His normally neat attire was wrinkled and dirty.

"Did run into Umbra or one of the other groups?" Harley asked.

"Yes," said Cain. "My own." He stepped past Harley and Kenyon and settled on one of the benches. Even his movements seemed tired and weak.

Kenyon shook his head. "That doesn't make any sense. Why would you be fighting with your own group?"

"Because of the aid I've given to Ms. Davisidaro and Mr. Templer," said Cain. He tipped back his hat and ran his fingers through his limp hair.

"You got hurt because of me and Noah?" said Harley. "But why? I thought you were only following your orders."

Cain nodded. "For the most part, I have been. However, in the matter of your confinement by Umbra, it seems I may have overstepped my boundaries." Cain paused for a moment and drew a deep breath. "I sent an agent into Umbra in an attempted escape."

Harley was surprised. "I didn't know that. I never saw any agent."

"That's understandable," Cain replied. "The agent was killed. Besides, I didn't send her to retrieve you. Her instructions were to bring Noah out and leave you behind."

"What?" Harley exclaimed. "You were going to get Noah out and leave me to be thrown in the pit?"

Cain leaned back and tipped his hat down to cast a shadow over his long face. "Yes," he said. "I wasn't sure what Umbra was going to do with you, but that wasn't my primary concern. I was only out to get Noah."

Harley didn't know what to say. She felt too much shock to even start to be angry.

Kenyon broke the silence. "What made Templer so valuable?" he asked.

"He had no value to me," said Cain. "But he had great value to Umbra. They hoped to use him in overcoming the problem of the spheres, and that had to be stopped at all costs."

"Spheres?" asked Harley. "You mean like the ones we saw back in Stone Harbor?" Floating spheres of light had appeared several times. One of them had even burned down Noah's house.

Cain nodded. "Yes. Though the spheres that both Umbra and Unit 17 have been hoping to generate are far more powerful than what you've seen." He paused and templed his long fingers together in front of his face. "Spheres are generated by mental powers. You can think of them as sort of a telepathic shout. In their simplest form, they can act as a remote viewer, letting the creator watch events from far away. More powerful spheres possess high levels of energy. They can be used to manipulate objects."

"Like burning down a house," said Harley.

"Yes. Fire is one of their most common abilities." Cain paused again and raised his hands to his long chin. He rubbed his face, producing a soft buzzing sound as his fingers slid over days of unshaved stubble. "But the most interesting property of the spheres is that they form a link—a connection—between two distant points in space."

It took Harley a moment to think through what the agent had said. "That's what they're after? A machine that can move things between one place and another?"

"Exactly," said Cain. "Though the spheres that can be generated by one person working alone aren't strong enough to allow a physical object to pass through. That's what is meant by the problem of the spheres."

Harley frowned. "I don't see why letting Umbra solve this problem would have been so bad. So they get a way to travel fast. So what?

"Are you kidding?" Kenyon asked her harshly. "What do you think these guys want to use this thing for, saving on airline costs?" He stood up and paced quickly around the circle. "Don't you understand what a *weapon* that would be?"

"Weapon?" Harley shook her head. "How could just moving things around make a weapon?"

"Quite simply," Cain said. "How could an army stand if their commander might be snatched away at any moment? Who could feel safe when an enemy agent might appear in their bedroom at any moment? What country could defend itself when a nuclear weapon might vanish from its silo and reappear inside the halls of Congress?"

A chill swept over Harley. "They could do that?"

"That and more," Cain replied. He stood up and stretched his long frame, then dropped back onto the bench. "Which is why it was essential that I remove Noah from Umbra's control."

Harley wasn't ready to forgive Cain for leaving her behind, but she could understand why Noah had to be taken out. The thought of such a power in the hands of people like Billie was too terrible to consider. "Why were you arguing with your own people?" she asked. "Because the agent was killed?"

Cain shook his head. "They are not concerned with my failure. They are concerned with your success."

Harley frowned. "What do you mean?"

"Your escape from Umbra resulted in a tremendous loss to the organization. They are weaker now than they have been in centuries." Cain reached into his pocket and pulled out an object that looked like a pen. Harley knew from experience that the small device was actually a powerful weapon. "My organization fears that Unit 17 or Legion will take this opportunity to smash what remains of Umbra."

Harley snorted. "Smash away," she said. "And good riddance."

Cain shrugged. "Personally, I am inclined to

agree. Of all the groups operating behind the curtain of secrecy, Umbra has always been the one that I feared most."

"But your bosses don't agree," Kenyon said, still pacing around the circle.

"My *associates* fear that once the competition has been eliminated, the path to ultimate power will be open." Cain tumbled the pen weapon around in his long fingers. "In short, you have upset the balance."

Anger tightened Harley's jaw. She got to her feet and stood in front of Cain. "They can all go to . . . well, to that pit in Umbra's cave," she said. "I can forgive you for not coming to save me. I'm not your responsibility. But I'm not going to apologize for what Noah and I did in there. We were only trying to survive."

Cain looked up at her from under the brim of his hat. "That was the position I took. But there was little agreement." The tumbling of the pen stopped. "In fact, my orders were to eliminate both you and Noah before you do any further harm."

Harley looked at Cain's hands and saw that the business end of the pen weapon was pointed straight at her face. "Eliminate?"

She heard a solid mechanical click from across the room. "Drop it, Cain," said Kenyon.

"Relax, Mr. Moor," the agent told him. "I have already refused to obey those orders." He nodded toward Harley. "If I wanted Ms. Davisidaro dead, we would not be having this conversation."

A loud ringing filled the room. Harley jumped and looked down at her chest, expecting to see some terrible wound.

"It's my cell phone," Kenyon said over the noise. He shoved his pistol back into his jacket and pulled out the small phone. "What?" He listened for a moment, then cursed under his breath. "All right," he said. "Don't bother with the apologies. Just follow the plan." Kenyon flipped the phone closed and shoved it angrily back into his coat.

"What's wrong?" asked Harley.

"Braddock escaped."

"How did *that* happen?"

Kenyon sighed and closed his eyes momentarily. "Apparently," he began, "Scott and Dee were . . . ahem . . . *busy* together, and not watching our prisoner. When they checked on Braddock, he had somehow sliced through the tape, and had vanished."

Cain stood up. "Braddock only let you take him prisoner," he said. "That should have been obvious."

Kenyon stepped in front of the tall agent and glared up at him. "You weren't there. How do you know?"

"Braddock is the regional commander of Unit 17. You really think he'd be taken so easily?"

"We had a plan," Kenyon insisted. "We worked hard to . . ."

As Kenyon and Cain argued, Harley felt an odd tickling at the back of her head. She staggered, then slumped down on the bench. Sparks gathered at the corners of her vision, and a strange hissing filled her ears.

Harley.

The voice in her mind came and went in an instant, but she had no doubt about the owner. "Noah," she whispered. "Noah, where are you?"

The reply came not in words, but in images. A

dizzying series of scenes flipped through Harley's mind like a high speed slideshow playing inside her skull. In a matter of seconds, she saw large hallways with white arched ceilings, then an incredible array of strange animals, glittering jewels in glass cases, huge ancient artifacts of wood and stone, and crowds of people. When the last image faded, the tickling in her head went with it.

Harley stood up. Kenyon and Cain were still facing each other a few feet away.

"Nobody is going to take a shot with a Taser just for the fun of it!" shouted Kenyon.

"I didn't say it was for fun," Cain replied calmly. "Braddock was willing to take some pain to promote the interests of Unit 17."

Harley stepped between the two and pushed them apart. "You guys can finish this later. We're leaving."

"Leaving?" Cain asked, surprised. "I haven't finished telling you everything you need to know."

"Later," said Harley. She started for the door.

"Where are you going in such a hurry?" Kenyon called after her.

"Yes," Cain said. "I would like to know that as well."

Most of the time, Cain seemed to know everything that was going on, but this time Harley was one step ahead of him. She paused at the door and looked back at the agent with a smile. "I'm going to pick up Noah," she said.

Noah peeked through the door of the grass hut and watched as two women pushed a baby carriage along the tile outside, until they disappeared behind a war canoe and a grove of palm trees.

For the next few minutes, Noah stayed inside the hut. It was a comfortable enough spot, with some simulated hides on the floor. He had to share the space with a model of a Pacific Islander who sat cross-legged in the doorway, but there was still plenty of room to stretch out and rest.

He wished he could know if his message to Harley had reached her. Breaking through the barriers that Ripley had placed around his mind had freed Noah's abilities, but his powers had not fully recovered. He could see the glow that came from people, and he could catch the occasional glimpse of the past or future. But the rest of his talents seemed out of reach or very weak. Just trying to contact Harley had left him feeling like he had run a mental marathon.

The lights in the hall dimmed. Noah closed his eyes and watched as a pale greenish glow slowly approached. He crowded back against the wall of the hut, getting as deep into the shadows as he could. The soft hiss of a broom came from outside as the janitor went past. Noah opened his eyes and peeked

139

through a gap in the wall in time to see the blue uniform move out of view.

His stomach grumbled. Getting into the natural history museum had been free, but the food was not. Noah couldn't remember if he had actually eaten in the fake hospital room. He couldn't remember the last time he had eaten at all.

Noah closed his eyes and turned his head slowly back and forth. Nothing. Cautiously, he squeezed through the entrance to the hut and stepped out into the display. A group of statues representing early Polynesians stood around a cold fire. A little further along the curve a larger hut sheltered a dozen more statues.

After another quick check at the entrance to the exhibit hall, Noah stepped out onto the balcony which circled the second floor. His plans for the night were very simple: find some food, find a place to sleep, and try again to communicate with Harley.

The gift shop at the top of the stairs was a disappointment. There was a metal gate blocking the entrance to the shop. Noah's mouth watered as he spotted candy bars on the shelf beside the register. But the array of chocolate and nuts was out of reach. He would have to keep searching.

He went over to the railing and looked down. With his eyes open, he could see nothing. But once they were closed, he spotted the glow from two figures moving on the ground floor. As quietly as he could, Noah snuck down the stairs and crouched behind a great pillar of stone. He waited until both of the people on the ground floor were off in a side gallery, then dashed out to hide behind the stuffed body of a huge elephant.

From where he stood, Noah could see the entrance to the cafeteria. Unlike the giftshop's, this door was wide open.

"There's got to be something left in there," he whispered to himself. He peeked between the elephant's legs. He saw no sign of the guards. Noah turned and dashed across the marble floor into the cafeteria. He made it without being spotted and breathed a sigh of relief.

Then the door at the far side of the cafeteria burst open and Commander Braddock stepped in. "Hello, Noah," he said. "Are you surprised to see me?"

Noah stared in shock as a dozen Unit 17 soldiers poured from the door.

"How did you find me?" Noah asked weakly.

Braddock tapped his finger against his temple. "Did no one ever tell you that exercising your mind leaves footprints behind? You've been shooting up flares, my boy. You shouldn't be surprised if someone saw them."

Noah swallowed a knot of fear in his throat. "What are you going to do now?"

"Absolutely nothing," said the Unit 17 commander. He sat down at a table and crossed his legs. "Your friend Harley will be along in a moment, and she has the device we want. When she gets here, we'll take you, her, and the device all at the same time." He ran his finger across his gray mustache. "A very neat solution."

A ripple of cold shot up Noah's spine. If his message had gotten through to Harley, then she would be following it right into a trap. He shook his head quickly. "Harley's not coming."

"Isn't she?" Braddock smiled. "Have a seat. Let's wait and see." When Noah didn't immediately move, the smile disappeared from the commander's face. "I said, have a seat," he repeated in a much firmer tone. Two of the soldiers came forward with their weapons drawn.

A crushing weight of despair settled over Noah. After escaping both Umbra and Legion, he had done nothing but land back in the hands of Unit 17—the same organization he had fought back in Stone Harbor. Reluctantly, he moved toward the nearest table.

"What's going on in here?" asked a new voice.

Noah turned and saw a security guard standing in the entrance to the cafeteria. The man had a gun in one hand and a walkie-talkie in the other.

"Get back!" Noah warned.

Instead of taking the advice, the guard stepped forward. "This museum is closed," he said. "How did you people get in here?"

"I have a key," said Braddock.

The guard seemed surprised. "You do?"

Braddock nodded. "Certainly. And here it is." He raised a knobby, thin-barreled gun.

Noah heard a whining sound that reminded him of an power drill. With the sound, a razor-thin line of glistening metal shot out from the gun. The line sliced through the security guard as cleanly as a sword splitting open a melon. A spray of blood erupted into the air. An arm—cut free at the elbow—fell to the marble floor.

The man's knees buckled and he fell facedown. The sheer amount of the blood was astounding.

Noah didn't wait to see more. He turned and ran.

"Stop him!" shouted Braddock. "Wound him if you can. Kill him if you must, but *stop* him!"

Again, Noah heard the power drill whine. Chips of stone flew from the floor beside Noah. Sparks raced along the wall.

He dodged around the big elephant. He heard a dull thump as shots cut into the thick hide of the dead beast. Boot heels thumped across the floor as the Unit 17 soldiers raced after Noah.

A shot glanced off a brass rail and Noah winced in pain as a sliver of metal lanced into his cheek. Warm blood spilled down his face. He dodged right to put one of the stone columns between himself and the men, then zigged back to the left through the opening into the hall of dinosaurs.

The skeletons of ancient giants loomed over Noah as he searched for some escape from the hall. The mad whine of the Unit 17 guns sounded again and again. The ribs of a huge Apatosaurus broke into a shower of black bone. Another burst cut through the frill of a Triceratops.

Noah dived for cover behind a display. Above him a glass case exploded. Fragments of rare fossils and jagged shards of glass flew together across the room.

Blasts cut through the pillar behind Noah. A severed electrical cable snapped and whirled around his head like an angry rattlesnake.

"Fan out," shouted one of the soldiers. "He's unarmed. Flank him and take him."

Noah rolled left. A stream of shots followed him that was so dense it dug a trench in the floor. He got to his feet and charged on into the hall of mammals.

Shots broke the cases on all sides. The flippers of an ancient whale were reduced to powder. With a groan, the long-dead animal tore free from the ceiling and came crashing down. A section of curving rib bone caught Noah on the shoulder and drove him to his knees. He started to get up, only to be hit again by the animal's massive skull.

Stars swam across Noah's vision that had nothing to do with paranormal abilities. He stood up for a moment, then fell back to his knees. Behind him he could hear the soldiers approaching. He closed his eyes against the dizziness and rose slowly to his feet. Noah wanted to scream with frustration. Once again, he was about to be captured. He was trapped.

Hands reached up and pulled him back down. "Stay on the floor," said a familiar voice. "It's safer down here."

Noah blinked in surprise. "Harley? What are you doing here?"

The words were barely out of his mouth when a bolt of blue white lightning shot through the hall. From back in the dinosaur hall came cries of alarm. As soon as the lightning faded, Noah heard a fast *boom, boom, boom* from a heavy pistol.

Harley looked at Noah and grinned. "I brought the cavalry," she said.

To Harley, the next few minutes seemed like a scene from a terrible nightmare.

The dark skeletal forms of huge beasts towered over the room, casting even darker shadows across the floor. The Unit 17 soldiers scurried like rats between the still forms of extinct monsters. As the soldiers moved, they sent blasts of impossibly fast needles scorching through space to crack walls, shatter glass, and carve metal. The mad whir of the sliver guns filled the air.

Cain's weapon answered with searing bolts of lightning that turned everything they touched into clouds of black soot. The leg of some looming prehistoric monster vanished in a flash. The creature fell with a noise like pianos crashing down a staircase, spreading fragments of ancient bone in all directions.

Harley clung to Noah and kept her face against the cold floor. Cain had warned her on the drive over that if shooting started, she should keep her head low. Harley had absolutely no problem with that advice. If there had been a way to dig a pit in the museum's marble floor, she would have been digging.

Noah inched forward and brought his face close to Harley's. "You heard me," he said, speaking loudly to be heard over the crash of weapons.

"I heard you." Harley slid a hand to Noah's face and touched the trickle of blood that ran across his cheek and dripped from the angle of his jaw. "You're hurt."

Noah laughed. "I'm alive. That's more than I expected."

One of the Unit 17 soldiers charged into the hall of mammals. His gun smashed the skull of a long-dead rhinoceros.

A lightning bolt caught the man right in the middle of the chest. He had time for a single scream before he was gone in a burst of flame. What was left was a cloud of greasy ash and an awful smell of burning flesh.

Amazingly, the firing from the Unit 17 soldiers increased. The whine of their guns merged into the buzz of a swamp full of giant mosquitoes. The streams of needles mowed down one fossil specimen after another, clipped off metal hand rails, and brought down showers of shattered glass.

Cain stuck his head from around a pillar of black onyx and sent a twisting rope of fire at the soldiers. Then he said something so amazing that Harley almost laughed. "Get ready to move."

"Are you kidding?" asked Harley. At the moment, the fire was coming so thickly that she wondered how long she could hold up a finger before it would be clipped off.

"I never kid," Cain replied bluntly. He stretched his hand above Harley and sent another burst of lightning toward the Unit 17 soldiers. "My weapon doesn't have an infinite supply of energy. If we stay here, we'll soon be overwhelmed."

From further back down the hall, Kenyon leaned out and fired a thundering shot from his pistol. "I'm down to about half a dozen shots," he warned. "If we're going to cut and run, now is the time."

"All right," Harley agreed reluctantly. "Let's get moving."

The first part of their retreat could not have been called running. Harley and Noah kept their face and stomachs flat against the floor as they crept away. Only their fingers and the tips of their toes moved them along. Fragments of broken glass cut into Harley's hands and arms as she crawled slowly past Cain's hiding place. Chunks of chipped stone and shattered bone ground against her ribs as she slipped past Kenyon. By the time she moved around the corner where she could stand up, she was bleeding from two dozen small wounds.

Noah joined her a moment later. He climbed to his feet and leaned against the wall. "Do you guys have a plan for getting out of here?"

Harley shook her head. "We didn't even have a plan for getting in. We broke in through the back and were searching for you when we heard all the noise."

She heard a final bark from Kenyon's pistol, and then he dashed around the corner. "How many?" he demanded.

"What?" asked Harley.

Kenyon's shook his head. "Not you, him," he said, nodding at Noah. "How many soldiers?"

Noah shrugged. "I'm not sure. Maybe a dozen."

Kenyon's dark eyes glittered. Harley saw an unpleasant flat expression on his face that reminded her of how he had looked when he had aimed the Taser at Braddock.

"Kenyon—" Harley started, but he cut her off with a wave of his hand.

"Cain got two," he said in a low voice. "I think I got another one. That leaves at least nine." He pressed a button on the handle of his gun and the ammo clip popped out. "Four in the clip and one in the chamber. That's not enough."

Harley touched him on the arm. "Kenyon, you can't shoot them all."

Kenyon whirled on her and slammed the clip back into his pistol. "I can try," he snarled.

Harley saw a blinding flash from around the corner as Cain fired a burst from his small weapon. A moment later, the agent appeared around the corner. His fedora hat was missing and there was a smoking hole in his flapping trenchcoat, but otherwise Cain appeared unharmed.

"Move," he said in a coarse whisper. He raised his pen weapon and pointed down the hallway. "That way."

Harley ran ahead of the others as they hurried past fossils of ancient fish and exotic invertebrates. She skidded to a halt at the end of the exhibit and peered around the corner. A giant inflatable spider guarded the entrance into the next hall, which housed the museum's insect zoo. The space didn't provide much cover. Harley saw only a series of aquariums raised on platforms of black plastic. But as far as she could tell, Unit 17 had not yet reached this room.

Noah pulled up beside her, followed by Kenyon and Cain.

"It looks clear ahead," said Harley.

Cain nodded. "Good. Through here, then into

the zoology hall on the other side. I'm going to stay here for a moment and slow them down. Now go!"

Harley sprinted between the legs of the inflatable spider. She dodged left at a tank of huge cockroaches, then right around a colony of termites. She was almost across the room when a form in dark blue leaped out from behind a display.

Harley shouted a warning and ducked under the man's arms. She felt a searing pain on her scalp. She tried to turn her head, but the man's fingers were buried in her hair. Harley grabbed the soldier's wrist and drove her nails into his flesh.

The grip on her hair only tightened. The Unit soldier spun her around, then delivered a stinging backhand to her face that left Harley's ears ringing.

"Be still," the man barked at her. "And you—"

Whatever the soldier was about to say, it was lost when a shot from Kenyon's pistol punched through the side of the man's chest. Harley stared in horror as the soldier's mouth dropped open, and let out a stream of dark blood along with a low, hopeless gasp. Then his eyes rolled up into his head and he fell.

Harley pulled free from the dead fingers and stepped back. Her heart was beating in her ears and her breath came in deep gasps.

"Now there are only eight," said Kenyon.

Harley heard a strangled cry to her left. She turned to see a second Unit 17 agent wrestling with Noah beside one of the insect cases. Kenyon raised his gun, but Harley shoved his hand away. "Don't!" she shouted. "You could hit Noah."

The Unit 17 agent was not as tall as Noah, but his

arms here heavy with muscle. Noah drove an elbow into man's chest and got a grunt in response. For a moment, Harley thought Noah was going to break free. But then the soldier wrapped an arm around Noah's throat and jerked him off his feet.

Harley didn't wait to see more. She ran forward, snatched up a small aquarium from the nearest stand, and brought it down over the skull of the soldier.

The man shoved Noah away and turned toward Harley. His left hand whipped up, displaying the heavy, sharp-nosed form of a sliver gun. "That was a very bad idea," he said. He raised the gun and pointed it at Harley's face.

Harley threw her hands up and took a step back, expecting the flurry of metal needles that would end her life.

But instead of firing, the soldier suddenly twitched and cried out in pain. He slapped at his own face with his right hand, then dropped the gun to the floor and slapped at his back with his left hand. Something small and reddish brown ran across the man's face, and he screamed. Another of the tiny creatures appeared on his shoulder, and Harley realized what it was—a scorpion.

The tank she had smashed over the man's head had been full of scorpions. Dozens of the creatures swarmed over the soldier, stinging blindly at his neck, face, shoulders, and hands.

The Unit 17 soldier tore open the front of his blue uniform and beat at something on his chest. White foam spilled from his lips, and his face swelled rapidly to the size of a basketball. His hands grew puffy and his eyes bulged in their sockets. He ran madly across the room, gave a final strangled cry, and fell with a lifeless thud.

Kenyon walked in front of Harley, bent down, and picked up the sliver gun from the ground. He straightened and offered the gun to Harley. "Only seven left now," he said.

Harley took the gun from his fingers without even thinking about it. She was still looking in horror at the fallen soldier. Tiny dark forms hugged the body. They struck again, and again, planting their stings in flesh that was already dead.

"Come on," called Noah. "We need to get on across."

"Right," Harley whispered. She took a step, and something crunched under her foot. Harley winced, but she followed Noah into the hall of modern zoology.

The three of them were only a few yards into the hall when Harley saw a pair of flashes from the other side of the insect zoo. Cain appeared from across the open space. He was running hard, and from the whining sound of the sliver guns, he was not far ahead of the remaining Unit 17 forces.

"Go on," he shouted as he charged toward them. "Keep moving!"

Harley turned and started down the hallway. This time Noah led the way, with Kenyon and Harley falling in behind. The sliver gun felt strange in Harley's hand, and she was careful to keep her fingers away from the trigger. The last thing she wanted to do was accidentally blow her own head off—or kill one of her friends.

Stuffed mammals of all kinds lined the wide hall-way. Harley passed a enormous snarling tiger, and a whole pride of lions. A Kodiak bear loomed out of the darkness, looking almost as large as the skeletons of dinosaurs. She noticed apes, and seals, and a rather pitiful looking kangaroo.

"Almost there," Noah shouted from ahead. "I can see an exit sign."

Harley felt a surge of hope. Maybe they were going to get out of this alive after all.

Then the stuffed raccoon she was running past exploded into sawdust and scraps of fur.

Harley threw herself to the ground as Unit 17 soldiers came boiling into the hall. Kenyon turned and fired his last three shots over Harley's head, but the soldiers didn't even seem to notice. They came forward at a run. Streams of needles cut the head from a stuffed gorilla and sent it rolling along the hall like some horrible bowling ball. The armor of a stuffed armadillo was no protection against the high velocity metal weapons. The little creature dissolved under a stream of shots. A single glass eye bounced on the marble floor, close to Harley's face.

One of the soldiers sent a stream of fire into the lights overhead. Darkness fell over the hall, broken only by showers of sparks and the flash of Cain's weapon.

Harley got on her feet and took a few steps. In the darkness and confusion, she couldn't see Noah or Kenyon. She was no longer even sure which was the right way to the exit.

Behind her, Cain fired another blast from his pen

gun. For a moment the hallway was lit by its brilliant blue-white glow. In that moment of light, Harley saw someone crouched only a few feet away, but she couldn't tell if it was Noah or Kenyon or one of the Unit 17 soldiers. Then the darkness returned, leaving only an afterimage behind.

Cain fired again. He was closer now, and Harley heard the agent's approaching footsteps over the whir and whine of the sliver guns.

"Over here," she called to him.

Her words attracted a fresh blast of needles. Harley ducked down as shots ripped into the walls and shattered a cabinet full of tiny mice and shrews.

Cain came up beside Harley, turned, and fired again. The power of his weapon had definitely weakened. The bolt he fired was pale and thin. "Come on," he said. His voice was hoarse and breathless. "Keep moving."

Harley stood up and turned to run. At that moment she heard a grunt, and something fell against her.

Her first thought was that it was another soldier attacking. She jumped back and raised the weapon in her hand, fumbling for the trigger.

But what she saw in the dim light was agent Cain. He was slumped on the floor with his arms spread. Harley ran back to him and knelt down at his side. There was a dark pool around his legs. Though it was too dark to see color, Harley had no doubt the pool was blood.

"Go on," Cain said weakly. "Leave me."

Harley felt a moment of temptation. Cain had sent an agent to get Noah out of Umbra's lair, but he had not helped Harley. She didn't owe him anything. She could run away and leave him here to be captured.

But that temptation faded quickly. "I'm not some big organization," she said, "and I don't try to figure out which people are worth saving."

Harley grabbed Cain by the shoulder and turned him over. A stream of needles had cut into his leg, tracing a line through his thigh and down to his knee. From the amount of blood he had lost, she was afraid the needles had split a major artery.

A blast of needles went past Harley's head so closely that she could hear the tortured scream of air rushing out of the way. Anger coursed through her. She raised her own sliver gun and pulled the trigger.

Nothing happened.

"Safety lock," whispered Cain. "You've got to have an implant in your hand to use one of those."

Harley spotted Cain's pen gun on the floor. She hurled the useless sliver gun into the darkness and picked up the small weapon. Placing her fingers on the two raised studs on the side of the tube, she fired.

The lightning was even weaker this time. It looked almost harmless as it trickled away down the corridor and faded in midair. By its bluish light, Harley saw a half dozen Unit 17 soldiers drawing closer. And she saw something else—Cain's blood was green.

She looked down at the agent in horror. "What are you?"

"Human," he replied. "The same as you."

Something hard pressed against the back of Harley's head. "Drop your weapon!" ordered a firm voice. "Now!"

Reluctantly, Harley let the pen weapon fall from her hand. She had no more tricks, no more places to run. Braddock had her now, and he would do whatever he wanted. She bent her head in despair.

The soldier gave the little pen weapon a hard kick and sent it skittering across the floor. Another soldier approached. And a third. In a moment, Harley and Cain were surrounded.

"We have the girl!" called one of the soldiers. He glanced down, and sent a sharp kick into Cain's injured leg. "And one of the others too."

A spark of the anger broke through Harley's gloom. "Leave him alone," she said. "He's injured."

The comment earned her a stinging slap. "Shut up," said the soldier.

Braddock appeared out of the darkness with a flashlight in his hands. He looked down at Harley and nodded. "Very good." Then he shown his light down at Cain. "Well, this is a surprising bonus. The famous Mr. Cain, actually taking action into his own hands. Or did you bring these children to do all the work?"

Cain stared up at him without answering.

"No matter," said Braddock. "It's going to be wonderful to get you back to our base and see what kind of wonderful stories you can tell." He pulled a small object from the pocket of his uniform and waved it above Harley. "Hmm. How disappointing. She doesn't seem to be carrying the device."

"Should we kill her now?" asked the soldier.

Braddock seemed to consider this for a moment. "No," he said. "I believe we can put them to immediate use. Get the girl on her feet."

Two of the soldiers dragged Harley from the ground and held her roughly between them. Braddock shined the flashlight in her eyes. He brushed her hair out of her face with his callused hand. "Smile, my dear. This is a very important role."

Harley pulled away from his touch in disgust. "Take your hands off of me."

Braddock grabbed her chin in his hand and squeezed her face painfully. "I'll do with you as I want," he snapped. "You're mine now."

The commander released his grip on Harley's face and turned to face the darkness. "You out there!" he shouted. "I have Ms. Davisidaro. If you do not throw down your arms and surrender yourself to my men within the next five seconds, I will make her a very pretty corpse."

There was no reply.

"Five!" announced Braddock.

Still nothing.

"Four!"

Harley struggled in the grip of the soldiers. "Get away!" she called into the darkness. "Run before he—," A hand clamped down on Harley's mouth, cutting off her words.

"Three!" shouted Braddock. "It will be a real shame to see the contents of this young lady's skull sprayed across this hall. But then, this is a place for dead things. What is one more, heh? Two!"

From surprisingly close by, Kenyon stood up. "Wait!" he called. "I'm right here."

"Drop your weapon!" ordered one of the soldiers.

Kenyon let the ugly Glock pistol clatter to the floor. "It was empty anyway," he said in a low voice. "If I had still had bullets, you'd all be dead."

"Brave words," sneered Braddock. "Losers are always full of brave words." He nodded to one of the soldiers. The man grabbed Kenyon and dragged him closer to Cain and Harley.

"Why didn't you run?" Harley whispered. "You didn't have to get caught."

Kenyon shrugged. "You're an asset."

Harley looked into his eyes. Kenyon might still be talking like an accountant, but he had risked his life to save her. "Thanks," she said.

Braddock directed his flashlight down the hallway, shining it over the still forms of two stuffed leopards and a puma mounted in the act of leaping. "Now who else do we have out there?" he called. "Mr. Templer, are you still in earshot?" The commander waited a moment, then shrugged. "Whether you can hear me or not, your time is at an end."

Braddock turned back toward Harley. "Greerson. Take Ms. Davisidaro aside and shoot her."

"Yes, Commander!"

One of the soldiers put his hand around the base of Harley's neck and squeezed painfully. "Come with me."

"No!" came a shout from far down the hallway. Noah Templer stepped into the light with his hands raised. "Don't shoot, I'm coming."

Two soldiers ran out to hustle Noah back to the others. He went straight to Harley and tried to hug her, but the Unit 17 men pulled them apart.

"This is not the time or place for sentiment," said Braddock. He shined the flashlight into Noah's face. "Are you the last?"

"Yes," said Noah, squinting against the light.

"And what about the device?" asked Braddock. "Where will I find the Trans-alpha amplifier?"

Harley pressed her lips together. As long as Unit 17 didn't have the device, there was at least a hope that they might at least make a deal. "Let the others go," she said. "And I'll take you to the device."

Commander Braddock only laughed. "I have a much better idea." He pulled out his sliver gun and placed it under Kenyon's chin. "We played this game once from the other side, now let's see how you like it. You tell me where to find the device, or I blow this fellow's head all the way into the rare birds display."

"Don't do it, Harley," said Kenyon. "Don't give it to them."

Braddock pressed the barrel of his gun upward, forcing Kenyon to tip his head back. "Five."

"Don't bother," Harley said. She took a deep breath and closed her eyes in resignation. "The orb is in the van. It's parked right outside."

"Wonderful," said Braddock. He clapped his hands together and smiled so broadly that the flashlight glinted from his teeth. "Greerson, take Hollander and gather up as much of the dead as you can find. Then see that a tragic fire is set in the main electrical junction."

"Right away, sir." Two soldiers jogged away into the darkness.

Commander Braddock ran his finger along his gray mustache. "This really is turning out to be a wonderful day."

THIRTEEN

"What *is* this stuff?" asked Noah. The material around his wrists had been soft and sticky at first, like some kind of taffy. But the more he struggled, the harder it became.

The soldier at his side didn't answer, which didn't really surprise Noah. The soldier stared straight ahead, with his back rigid, his hands on his knees, and his mouth shut. He had not said a word since he had shoved Noah into the car and driven away. Noah was beginning to wonder if Unit 17 had started to build robots.

Harley had been loaded into another car, and Kenyon into a third. Cain, his wounded leg roughly bandaged, had been chosen for the dubious honor of riding with Commander Braddock. The line of dark sedans driving across the darkened city reminded Noah of the parade of secret service cars that drove around with the president—or the line of cars at a funeral.

The sedan moved out of Washington, out into the countryside. Ahead of them the sky turned purple, then pink, then blue. The bright yellow arc of the sun rose over the pine trees. It looked like it was going to be a beautiful winter day.

Noah leaned back in his seat and closed his eyes. The pain in his cheek and the aches in the rest of his body made it hard to concentrate, but as he drew in slow cleansing breaths, his powers began to gather.

The highway was covered in bits and pieces of

images from the past and future: cars rolled over onto their roofs, ambulances with their sirens blaring, jackknifed trucks and crying people sitting in the weeds at the roadside. As usual, it was the most traumatic, most terrible moments that left behind the clearest images. None of it was any use to Noah. He shoved away both the images and the babble of voices from the minds of passing motorists.

With his eyes closed, Noah turned his face toward the soldier at his side. The man was a pale, silver-gray color from head to toe. Unlike the other auras Noah had glimpsed, the Unit 17 soldier was all one color, absolutely smooth, like a house after a fresh coat of paint. The driver of the car looked the same. Even stranger, Noah could sense no cord leaving their bodies for the nexus. These men seemed to be completely unconnected to the great and complex knot of dreams that Noah had thought joined everyone. He sent his thoughts closer, trying to find out more about what made the soldiers so different from everyone else.

Pain whipped through Noah like an electric shock.

He gasped and opened his eyes. The soldier still sat there, eyes forward, back straight. If he had noticed of Noah's mental exploration, he didn't show it.

A machine. The man wasn't a robot, not exactly, but something had been planted in his mind that kept Noah from catching even a glimpse of the man's thoughts or emotions. Noah closed his eyes and pushed his thoughts out again. All the Unit 17 people were as blank and unreadable as stone. It went beyond protection. Something deeper had been done to them, something that made them as cold and unfeeling as any machine.

Noah shivered. Umbra had worked in dark caverns and practiced rituals with things that were so far beyond normal that he didn't even have the words to explain them. They were Evil. Not evil, like the people who robbed or killed on the evening news, but Evil, with a big *E*.

Compared to them, Unit 17 seemed like nothing special—a bunch of guys playing with high-tech toys, all shiny and digital.

But what these people did with their computers and technology was, in its own way, just as dark as any ancient ritual Umbra had practiced in its caves.

Noah's thoughts were interrupted as the car suddenly swerved into the right lane. An Air Force base slid past on the left, then there was a series of low buildings. At the next exit, the lead car in their little parade of prisoners peeled off the interstate. The rest of the vehicles followed as they looped around and drove down a two-lane road between pine trees that looked ready to be turned into telephone poles on a moment's notice.

Ten minutes later, they came to a stop. Noah leaned to the side so he could see around the driver.

He spotted a gate ahead, guarded by a man in a plain blue uniform. Beyond the gate Noah could see a new blacktop road leading between the trees. The gate rolled aside and the cars went in.

They passed a row of ranch houses on the left. Then a couple of small offices on the right. Something seemed terribly familiar about it all. A half mile further on, they came to an airstrip with two huge hangers on the far side.

"Tulley Hill," muttered Noah in surprise. "This is Tulley Hill." The Tulley Hill base outside Stone Harbor had been the place where Harley's father had disappeared. Noah and Harley had searched the base and had seen some of the experiments going on there. But only one day after a battle had destroyed part of the base, they had returned to find everything gone. Every building at Tulley Hill had completely disappeared.

Noah turned to the silent man beside him. "You moved it all here, didn't you?" The soldier glanced at Noah for a moment, then stared straight ahead again.

Ahead of the cars, a complex that was all too familiar appeared. Spires and domes rose up amid mushrooms and ridges of twisted metal. The building at the heart of the Unit 17 base had no straight lines or neat corners. It was as fluid and twisted as some immense organ ripped from an unbelievably huge body. Even the reddish and bruised purple colors of the walls looked like something living.

The line of cars stopped beside a wrinkled extension that reached into the parking lot like a tentacle. One by one, the doors popped open and the soldiers and their prisoners spilled out.

The soldier who had sat so still through the ride moved quickly to take control of Noah. He grabbed the bar of material that bound Noah's hands together and dragged him through the door. Then he led Noah over to join the others.

Kenyon was nearest to Noah. Noah noticed a new bruise on his face that hadn't been there at the museum. He suspected that Kenyon and his guard had shared more than a conversation on the way to the base.

Next in line stood Cain. The agent leaned against one of the Unit 17 soldiers. His face was pale, and his shoulders slumped, but Noah thought it was at least a minor miracle that Cain was alive at all.

At the far end of the line stood Harley. She looked across at Noah and raised an eyebrow. Her lips moved. Though Noah was too far away to hear the sounds, the words played in his mind. *What do we do now?*

Hang on, he sent back. *Look for our chance. Don't give up.*

Commander Braddock walked to the circular entrance at the end of the round extension. He had a satisfied smile on his face and the golden orb in his hand. "Gentlemen—and lady—welcome to Point Base Bravo."

"You know what you can do with your welcome," Kenyon snarled.

Braddock looked at him with a hard expression. "I've had a chance to review our records, Mr. Moor. I know who you are and what slights you hold against us." He walked over to Kenyon and leaned in so close that their noses were almost touching. "Now I want you to understand this—of everyone here, you are the most expendable. Give me any reason, and you will be terminated. Clear?"

Kenyon glared back at the commander. "Clear," he said through clenched teeth.

"Good." Braddock turned to the door and pressed his palm against a plate. The panel faded away like mist under a hot sun, revealing a curved hallway that snaked into the complex. "Bring them," said Braddock. Without looking back, he stepped inside.

Noah and the others were ushered through the round hallway and into the heart of the strange building. Just as it had at Tulley Hill, the hallway around them branched and changed color several times. Finally, they reached a corridor that curved upward in a long gradual slope. At the top of the slope, a door opened to reveal a place as familiar as Noah's nightmares.

They were standing near the top of a huge open room. It was a space wide enough to hold a dozen football fields and high enough to fit a medium-sized skyscraper without denting the roof. In the center of this vast space grew a forest of metal trees that reached upward like redwoods and wire vines that descended to wrap them in a jungle of cables. Clouds drifted through the space, lit from within by sparks of blue and red and green.

"I hope none of you suffer a fear of heights," said Braddock as they were escorted onto a platform at the edge of the drop. With a signal from the commander, the platform began to descend into the electric jungle.

As they dropped toward the forest of metal trees, the cables split and shrank from massive trunk lines thicker than Noah's body into dozens of cords the as big around as his finger, and finally to thousands of wires as fine as a hair. The metal trees grew gradually thicker, and the air hotter as they descended. Wisps of fog streamed around the edge of the platform.

The open elevator reached the ground, and they

were lead away between the massive trunks of the metal trees. Finally, at the very center of the vast room, they came at last to a raised platform flanked by banks of equipment that rose up in flowing projections and rippled wings. Pulses of colored light moved through the equipment like the pulse of a slow heartbeat.

"What is this place?" asked Kenyon.

Braddock put his hand against a rounded projection. A yellow glow gathered around his fingers. "You'll see very soon."

A woman with short black hair and pale skin came hurrying around the platform. "Commander! I didn't realize you would be here so soon." She smiled nervously.

"You should've realized by now that I don't waste time, Ms. Avondale." Braddock nodded toward the platform. "Have you prepared a place for the amplifier?"

The woman nodded. "Yes. We weren't really sure of the physical size, so we designed it to—"

"Spare me the details," Braddock interrupted. He placed the golden orb in the woman's hands. "Install that right away."

"Yes, Commander." The dark-haired woman took the orb as if it were made of glass—or high explosives. She moved carefully into the twisted wings and knobs lining the edge of the platform and placed the metal ball into a curved recess. At once, the pulse of colors in the machine began to move faster. "The amplifier is in place," the woman announced.

The commander turned to face Harley. "Now, Ms. Davisidaro, we come to the heart of the matter. As I told you earlier, it is our intention to retrieve your father."

Noah saw Harley's eyes narrow in suspicion. "Are you serious?" she asked.

"Absolutely." Braddock walked up a sloping ramp and stood on the white platform. "Your father was testing a device just like this one at Tulley Hill. He generated a transport sphere and entered it successfully, but our experiment was rudely interrupted before he could be retrieved. Now we need your help to get him back."

Harley shook her head. "Even if I believe you, why do you need *my* help?"

"Because we need someone with your powers," the commander explained. "To operate the device, we must have a source of Trans-alpha radiation. Your mother was gifted with the ability to produce this energy, and we believe that you have inherited her talent. With the amplifier to assist your output, you can generate the power we need."

As the commander talked, Noah received an image. He swayed on his feet. In many ways, it was the most awful image his talents had shown him, and it carried a feeling of absolute certainty.

Noah stepped away from his guard. "Wait," he called.

Braddock turned to him with an irritated look. "What is it, Mr. Templer?"

"Let me do it."

"Let you do what?"

"I can power your machine." Noah stepped onto the edge of the platform. "I volunteer."

FOURTEEN

"Noah!" Harley shouted. "You can't." She tried to step forward, but one of the soldiers held her arms.

"Don't worry," said Noah as he turned and smiled at her. "It'll be okay."

Harley thought of the secret hospital she had seen in New Jersey, and the woman who might be her mother. The woman was not okay. She was a long way from okay. "Don't do it, Noah," Harley urged. "You don't know what it might do to you."

Commander Braddock stepped up to Noah and smiled. "Splendid," he said. "We can save Ms. Davisidaro as a backup plan."

Harley again tried to push forward, but one of the soldiers held her back. "Don't do it!" she called to Noah. "That thing will kill you—or worse."

Braddock chuckled. "You had best hope that Mr. Templer handles this attempt well," he told Harley. "Should he prove inadequate to the task, you'll be next."

One of the soldiers tapped a brass-colored rod against the material binding Noah's wrists. The substance crumbled and fell away. Then the dark-haired woman lead Noah up a shallow ramp to a body-sized gap in the curving edge of the platform. Once again, the lights around the platform began to pulse more quickly. "This can't be," Ms. Avondale said in surprise. "He's generating Trans-alpha patterns off the charts."

"Wonderful," said Braddock. He rocked back and forth on his heels. "Give the orders. We are going to full power immediately."

The woman stepped down beside him. "Are you certain we should? We haven't tested the system with the amplifier. We're not certain of the appropriate levels. I've never seen this kind of power before."

Braddock scowled at her. "I've waited long enough for this. I'll not wait for weeks while you carry out endless tests. Go to full power *now*."

"Yes, Commander." The woman hurried away. Within moments, enormous arcs of lightning began to slam between the metal trees. The pulsing lights around the platform brightened and began to move so quickly that they became nothing but a blur.

Harley strained against the arms holding her back. "Noah, get out of there! *Please!*"

Noah only shook his head. "Wait," he called back. "I know what I'm doing." A pale greenish glow seeped from the cluster of wires and pipes and spread in a misty blanket over Noah's body. It grew paler and brighter with each passing moment.

Cain limped forward. "Stop this now, Braddock," he shouted. "While you still have a chance."

The commander laughed from his place on the white platform. "You think I'm afraid of your pitiful little group, Cain? Wait until this experiment is over. You and I will have plenty of time to . . . talk."

"It's not my group you should fear," said Cain.

A deep thrumming rose from underfoot. Lightning struck down from the tangled jungle of cables, and thunder pealed between the metal trees. Harley felt her hair lift as a breeze gusted around the platform.

Noah was invisible now, lost under a cloud of green so pale it was almost white.

"Look!" shouted Kenyon. "Is that one of the spheres you talked about?"

At the center of the platform a ball of light had appeared. It was small, no bigger than the golden orb, and its color was a deep, bloody red.

Harley nodded. "Yes. One like that burned down Noah's house."

The sphere grew larger. As it grew, its color began to change. It became orange, and then yellow.

Harley squinted as the light from the sphere intensified. She wished her hands were free so she could shield her eyes. The wind around her grew into a hurricane. The thunder above was a continuous drumroll. The lightning in the wires was a mad dance of fire.

Then the orb expanded suddenly from the size of a basketball to a width of ten feet or more. It shed all color and became as white as fresh snow.

The thunder stopped. The lightning paused. The great space was as abruptly silent as a tomb. In the center of the platform hung a white sphere. It seemed as smooth and still and as solid as a ball of stone.

From the edge of the platform Braddock applauded. "Marvelous! It's far more stable than anything we have established in the past. This is what we've been waiting for!" He stepped up onto the platform and walked around the floating sphere, examining it from all sides. "It's perfect. Simply perfect."

The dark-haired woman dashed around the platform after him. "We've matched the signature of the Tulley Hill event!" she announced excitedly. "We should have contact."

Braddock looked down at Harley. "Well, Ms. Davisidaro. Now we will see if your father is still in there."

Harley's heart leaped into her throat. "What . . . what is it like in there?"

"It's not like anything," answered the woman. She bent over a bank of flickering lights and tiny switches. "Our theories indicate that there should be no subjective experience within the sphere. It is essentially a zone of nothing. Pure emptiness."

Emptiness. Harley didn't know how to feel about that, or about anything else. She wished she could see Noah through the haze that surrounded his body. She wished she could know that he was all right.

For so long, Harley had wanted nothing but to find her father. Now she stood on the edge of getting him back, and she wondered if she was making a mistake.

The father she had loved all her life had lied to her. He had lied about his work and lied about what had happened to her mother. She missed her father desperately, but she wasn't sure she was ready to welcome the man she had discovered while he was away.

"We have movement!"

Harley squinted against the glare of the light. Something was shifting inside. It was hard to see any detail against the brightness of the sphere, but she thought she could see the movement of arms and legs. A figure took shape within the light. It was a man, a man with dark hair and a slim build.

"Daddy?" Harley choked out.

Frank Davisidaro stepped out of the light.

Though Harley's father had been gone only a few months, he looked so different that Harley almost didn't recognize him. He had always been a handsome man, with olive skin, jet-black hair, and a flashing smile. But as he stumbled away from the sphere his face was haggard, thin, and worn. His black hair was split by a streak of white. His clothing was torn and tattered.

Looking at him, Harley realized that she no longer cared about the lies, or about Unit 17, or about the sphere and how it might be used as a weapon. She had her father back. For now, that was all that mattered. "Dad!" she cried again. "Dad! Are you okay?"

Her father's head turned slowly toward her voice and he blinked. "Harley? Honey, what are you doing here? You've got to get away."

Commander Braddock stepped between them. "Your daughter was just helping us to extract you from your device, Doctor."

"Helping?" repeated Harley's father. His voice was full of confusion. He stood on the platform looking blankly at Braddock.

Harley struggled against the soldier holding her arms. "Let me go!" she shouted. "I've got to go to him!"

"Commander!" shouted the dark-haired woman. "We've got more movement in the field."

"Very good," said Braddock. He stepped past Harley's father and looked again into the white ball. "Now comes the real test."

From within the white sphere, Harley saw more movement. Once again, the figure of a man formed within the light. The man stepped out of the sphere. He was young, no more than twenty, and he wore the blue uniform of Unit 17. He staggered for a few steps and looked around in confusion. Then he spotted Braddock and snapped a crisp salute. "Robbins reporting, sir. I've just made the transition from site gamma. The gateway is functioning."

"Excellent, Robbins. I trust you had no trouble matching our signal?"

"None at all, sir."

Braddock smiled broadly. He turned and clamped a hand on Frank Davisidaro's shoulder. "Congratulations, your creation is a total success. We'll be able to put it to use right away."

Harley saw an expression of shock on her father's face. "No!" he shouted. "It's not a success." He shrugged off Braddock's hand. "I was wrong. Wrong about everything. You have to shut it down now and never use it again."

The commander frowned. "I'm afraid I don't agree with your assessment." He raised his right hand. In his hand Harley saw something bulging and ugly with a long thin barrel.

"No!" she shouted. A frozen moment followed her outcry—a second that stretched out for what seemed like hours. Harley kicked her heel into the shin of the soldier who held her, forcing the man to loosen his grip. From the corner of her eye, she saw Kenyon and Cain also fighting with the men who held them. Harley pulled away and ran two fast steps toward the platform before Braddock shot her father.

The sliver gun whined for only a moment, and the hole it punched through Frank Davisidaro's chest was tiny. But the effects for that hole were huge.

Harley's father staggered back a step, shivered, then crumpled to the floor.

"Dad!" Harley screamed. Then her voice rose up in a cry that had nothing to do with words. She managed another step, then her legs buckled and she fell to her knees as she looked at her father's body on the ground. The soldier caught up to Harley and grabbed her by the arms, but it did nothing to still her cries. She pulled in a deep breath and let out another howl of despair.

Braddock stepped over her father, pulled back his arm, and smashed the sliver gun across Harley's mouth. The blow brought a tremendous flash of pain, and sent Harley sprawling across the floor.

"Shut up," demanded Braddock, "or I'll arrange a more permanent reunion with your father."

Harley wiped blood away from her smashed lips and stared up at him through tears. "Why? she asked, her throat raw. "Why kill him now?"

Braddock strolled back to the platform and stood near the white sphere. "Your father was instrumental in the development of this technology," he called over his shoulder. "For years he contributed willingly, and for more years he worked to save your mother from the blunders he had made." The commander shook his head. "Unfortunately, your father's sense of morality began to interfere with his usefulness. In the last few years, only threats against his darling daughter drove him to continue. Now that the device is functional, there was no need to put up with him any longer."

"But he *can't* be dead," Harley insisted. She looked at the body lying on the floor beside the huge white ball. "This has to be a nightmare." She felt a tingling in her feet and a strange lightness in her head. She thought she might just blow away at any moment. She felt oddly sleepy. Maybe if she closed her eyes and waited, everything would go away.

"Believe what you will." Braddock gestured toward the orb. "Your father is gone, but as you can see, his theories have been put to good use. You should be proud."

The words were barely out of Braddock's mouth when lightning suddenly flashed between all the metal trees at the same time. The blast of thunder that followed stunned Harley and left her ears ringing like twin alarms.

Up on the platform, the sphere was larger. It was twenty feet across, so large that Braddock was forced to move back or be taken in by the white light.

"Ms. Avondale!" he shouted. "What is happening?"

The woman moved her hands frantically over the bumpy, irregular equipment. "Power output is up another thirty percent and still climbing."

"Bring it under control," instructed Braddock. "Insert the dampers."

"They're in!" Ms. Avondale called frantically. "Power up fifty percent."

A new wind rose in the chamber. Unlike the random breezes that had come before the sphere's creation, this wind blew straight into the growing white globe. Dangling wires above the platform leaned toward the light. Yards of cable vanished into the sphere like a kid sucking in spaghetti.

The surface of the white sphere was no longer smooth and flat. It began to boil and surge.

Sparks and flashes of color shot up from inside.

"It's unstable," shouted Braddock. "Shut it down! Shut it down *now!*"

More lightning crackled through the metal jungle. The thunder was almost continuous, as one explosive blast followed on the tail end of the last.

Ms. Avondale climbed past the place where Noah lay wrapped in light, and reached for the golden orb. A dozen arms of lightning snapped from the control panel, wrapping her body in snakes of blue fire. The woman screamed. Her eyes bulged in their sockets. Her skin smoked. Her crown of dark hair burst into flame. Then she was hurled away into the forest of electric trees.

The white sphere expanded again. Its glowing surface snagged the arm of the young soldier who had come through the sphere. He struggled to get away, a look of terror on his face. But like a man sinking into quicksand, his every motion only seemed to accelerate his being pulled into the sphere.

Harley watched it all with a feeling of numbness. Her father was dead. The guards that had been holding her arms released their grip. She barely noticed.

The sphere expanded again. It was no longer resting on the platform, it was *in* the platform. The woven ceramic plates of the floor cracked and crumbled into the glowing white mass. The wings of equipment at the edge of the platform creaked and bent inward.

Commander Braddock shouted some command, but Harley couldn't hear his words. He jumped from the edge of the platform and plunged down, his knees bent to absorb the impact of landing.

He never landed.

In midair, Braddock slowed to a stop. For a fraction of second, he hung there, suspended five feet above the ground. His gray eyes went wide with an expression Harley had never seen on the commander's face before—pure terror. Slowly, he was pulled back up, and in. With his mouth open in an unheard scream, Braddock vanished into the sphere.

A touch on her shoulder caused Harley to turn her head. She looked around to see that the guards had gone. Only Cain and Kenyon remained.

Cain put his mouth near Harley's ear. "Come on," he said. "We need to get out of here."

Harley shook her head and looked toward the platform. "We can't leave Noah," she cried. "And we have to get my father. He might . . . he might still be alive." She stepped toward the platform, fighting to stay on her feet against the raging wind. The hurricane blasts whipped Harley's hair around her face, and the brilliance of the sphere nearly blinded her. The place where Noah had been placed in the machine was now no more than a few feet from the edge of the expanding sphere. Her father's body was inches from the edge.

A sudden lull in the storm quieted the room. The sphere, now almost fifty feet across, grew still and calm. The wind faded to a breeze.

The white light above Noah's body vanished. With tremendous relief, Harley watched Noah pull himself free of the machine.

"Noah!" she shouted. "Get out of there before it starts again."

Noah finished extracting himself from the machine and hurried to Harley. He wrapped her in a fierce hug. "I'm sorry," he said, his voice full of sadness.

Harley wished she could hug him back, but her wrists were still held in the grip of the strange handcuffs. "It's not your fault," she said, looking over his shoulder at her father. She stepped back. "Come on, let's get my father and go before the sphere gets any bigger."

Noah shook his head slowly. "I'm not leaving. At least, I'm not going that way."

"What do you mean?" asked Harley, but there was a rising pain in her chest. She knew what he meant.

"They're wrong about it," said Noah. He turned to face the sphere. "It's not empty in there, Harley. It's *full*. There are whole worlds inside the sphere. And it's the only chance for your father."

"Chance?" Harley said in confusion. "He's dead. How can he have a chance?"

Noah tapped a finger against the side of his head. "I've seen it, Harley. Things aren't over yet. Not for me, or you, or for your father." He stepped back and bent down beside Mr. Davisidaro.

Harley felt a mixture of hope and turmoil. She hurried to join Noah. Her father's face was pale and still. There was no rise and fall of breathing in his chest. "Noah," she said softly. "You don't have to do this. If you go in, I don't know how to get you back."

Cain stepped forward. "She's right, Noah. You may be the only person in the world capable of opening such a portal. If you step in, there may be no way to get you out."

Noah shook his head. "Don't worry," he said. "I'm coming back." Then he turned to face Harley, his smile fading.

"Don't go," she pleaded.

"I have to," Noah replied. He quickly stepped forward and kissed her lips gently. "What might have been," he said softly.

If Harley's hands had been free, she would have encircled him in her arms and refused to let go. But all she could do was watch, tears streaming down her face, as Noah slipped his arms under Harley's father, and lifted the man's body from the floor. Then he stood and took a step into the sphere. Streamers of light swirled around the body in his arms.

"Noah!" Harley called after him. "Don't leave me. Don't leave me alone."

"You're not alone," Noah replied from the white glow. "Don't worry, Harley. I'll be back. I've seen it."

"Please," Harley begged. Her throat was raw with anguish. "Don't."

"I have to," Noah replied. He grinned at her. "See you when you least expect it."

With that, Noah spun around and stepped completely into the light.

The instant he vanished, a thunderclap slammed across the platform. The ball of light surged outward, growing to sixty feet in diameter, then seventy.

Harley took a step toward the light. She could go. She could join Noah and her father. If Noah was right, then anything could happen inside the sphere. Maybe her father was still alive after all. Maybe they could all be happy.

Something shoved Harley back. She tried again to take a step, and again she was shoved back. Irritated, she turned her head and saw Kenyon.

"Get away from that thing!" he screamed at her.

Harley shook her head. "I have to go with Noah."

"You heard him. He's coming back." Kenyon pushed Harley away from the sphere with his shoulder. "Come on!"

Reluctantly, Harley turned away from the sphere and followed Kenyon into the forest of metal trees.

Cain was already shuffling away, but he couldn't travel very fast on his wounded leg. Harley and Kenyon moved to his side, giving the agent something to lean against as he limped toward the exit.

Harley heard a tremendous groan from behind them. She glanced over her shoulder. The sphere had swelled to at least a hundred feet across. The nearest of the metal trees were bowing down, bending to meet the light.

Kenyon headed for the elevator platform, but Harley blocked his way. "Over here," she called over the rising wind. "There's a faster way out."

She led the way through the forest to the door that she and Noah had used when escaping the disaster at Tulley Hill. Behind them, the chorus of groans and crashes and squeals of ripping metal grew ever louder. Metal giants taller than any real tree that had ever lived buckled and fell into the light. High above, a portion of the ceiling ripped free and tumbled down into the whiteness. Sunlight spilled into the room, adding to the glare.

Harley was almost to the door when two figures stepped in front of them. The newcomers wore plain blue jumpsuits, but they didn't look like Unit 17 soldiers. One of them was tall and so skinny that the jumpsuit hung loose on his thin frame. The other was more than a foot shorter, with chin-length auburn hair framing a round face.

"Halt," said Dee. "Who goes there?"

Harley looked at her in shock. "What are you doing here?"

"Rescuing you," said Dee. "Do you want us to leave?"

Kenyon came up. For once, he looked as surprised as Harley. "But how did you get here?"

It was Scott that answered. "We picked up the Unit 17 radio transmissions and figured out what happened. Then I used the signal strength to figure out direction, and—"

Cain limped past them. "Explain later," he said. "Get out now."

"Where's Noah?" asked Dee. "Isn't he with you?"

Harley paused and glanced back again. The white sphere filled half the space in the huge room. She saw no sign of any human movement inside. "No. Noah's not with us." She turned and stepped out into the daylight.

The line of cars that had carried the prisoners to the base was gone. The only vehicle that remained in the parking lot was Kenyon's blue van.

"Didn't you have trouble getting in?" Kenyon asked as they climbed into the van.

"The only trouble we had was getting out of the way of people rushing out," replied Dee. "Everybody in this place was in a big hurry to leave."

"They had the right idea," said Cain. He fell onto the floor of the van and lay there. "Drive. Quickly."

Scott climbed behind the wheel and cranked the van's motor. "We'll be out of here in a flash."

"That's what I'm worried about," said Cain.

Harley watched through the back window as the van rolled out of the parking lot. The strange building with its spires and odd projections was swaying like grass in a high wind. Fissures tore through the metal hide, and shafts of white light emerged. Then the whole building was gone, leaving nothing but a white sphere easily a thousand yards across.

The sphere was growing faster. Harley could see it rising into the sky and eating away at the blacktop parking lot. By the time the van reached the airstrip, the sphere was half a mile wide, and growing faster every second.

"It's catching up to us," she warned. "Go faster!"

Scott poured on the gas, skidding the van along the curving street. The sphere expanded. It was too large now to even tell it was a sphere. All Harley could see was a great white wall, rushing toward them and swallowing trees, hangars, and buildings as it came.

Kenyon crawled to the back of the van and joined Harley at the window. "What do you—" his words faded off as he saw the approaching sphere.

"We're not going to make it," Harley said softly.

"We'll make it," said Kenyon.

The van sped on past the row of ranch houses. Harley glanced at the center house. She knew it was the same house she had lived in on the Tulley Hill base back in Stone Harbor. It was the last place she had lived with her father. She wondered for a moment if all the things she and her father had owned were still inside the house.

If she walked through the door, she might find her father's beloved books, her old track trophies, and the photo album that contained pictures of her mother.

The white wall rolled past the house, erasing it as if it had never existed.

"Good-bye, Dad," whispered Harley.

The sphere was only a hundred feet behind them when they reached the houses, and less than fifty feet behind when they rolled through the abandoned gates.

"Faster!" shouted Kenyon.

"I've got it floored already," Scott called back.

The white wall was thirty feet back. Twenty. Ten.

Faint pastel colors appeared in the whiteness. All at once, the sphere was becoming translucent, like a bubble of milky glass. It caught up to the van, rushed over it, and through it.

Harley felt a momentary sensation of falling, and another feeling she had never experienced before, a feeling of expanding, as if she was everywhere in the sphere at once. Then the wall was past, dissipating into the air.

From fifty feet behind the van, to as far as Harley could see, there was nothing. The Unit 17 base and the forest around it was gone. Every building and every tree had been swallowed by the white sphere. In their place was a curved depression in the earth that bared layers of sandstone and soil like the crater of some great meteorite.

At the center of the crater, where the sphere had been generated, Harley saw a tiny brilliant spark hover for a moment in the air. Then the spark was gone.

She laid her face against the cold metal side of the van and cried.

EPILOGUE

"Hold still," said Dee. "You wiggle like that again, and you won't have anywhere to put your gloves."

Harley nodded and tried to hold still as Dee sawed at the hardened putty holding her wrists. She stared off through the window.

Cain had directed them to a small cabin on the Virginia coast. The place was empty, but well stocked with food and supplies. It was a pretty spot, with waves rolling up onto tawny sand and old oak trees twisted by time and storms.

Harley barely saw it. In her mind was a single image: Noah walking into the light holding the body of her father. Despite what Noah had said, Harley felt terribly alone. She felt a shadow of anger with Noah. Her father had not been given a choice, but Noah had gone away through his own free will. Maybe Noah would find a way to save her father, and he might not. All that Harley was sure of was that for now she had lost them both.

And her father's journal had disappeared with Braddock into the sphere. She had even lost that small comfort.

The putty around Harley's wrists suddenly broke into a dozen pieces.

"Cool," said Dee. She stood up and waved her hacksaw. "Now to go cut free Mr. Kenyon Big Bucks." She took a couple of steps and then paused.

A wicked smile spread over her face. "Or maybe not. A few days without being able to comb his hair or change his shirt might be good for him." She walked off, still waving the saw.

Harley stayed where she sat. Tears were beginning to flow again, spilling from her eyes and running down her cheeks. It had been almost ten hours since the white sphere had taken Noah and her father, but Harley had cried for almost the whole time. It was embarrassing. She had never been a crier—she *hated* people that sat around and wept. But she just couldn't seem to stop.

The door to the cabin opened softly and Agent Cain stepped in. Though it had been less than a day since he was wounded, the tall man had already shown remarkable healing power. He was barely limping, and actually looked better than when Harley had met him in Washington D.C. He had even managed to find another fedora hat.

"I see you've been freed of your restraints," said Cain.

Harley wiped a tear from her cheek. "Yes," she said. She wished Cain would go away. She was in no mood to talk to him about secret organizations and world-shaking plots. What Harley wanted was her father back. She wanted Noah. She wanted to go *home*.

Cain pulled out a chair and sat down beside her at the small table. "What will you do now?" he asked.

Harley shrugged. "Does it matter?"

"I think it does. Where will you go?"

"Back to Stone Harbor, I guess." Harley sniffed back another tear. "Dee's father is probably going insane looking for her."

Cain nodded. "Officer Janes was certainly not thrilled with his daughter's departure. However, certain parties have kept him informed of her health."

"You?"

"My associates."

Harley looked into Cain's dark eyes. "You talk about these associates of yours, but I never seem to meet them."

"I believe you will," said Cain. He stood up and walked toward the door. "In good time."

"I'm in no hurry," said Harley.

Cain reached the door and started out, then he paused and looked at Harley from under the brim of his hat. "Do you remember telling me that you would destroy all of the secret groups?"

Harley nodded. "Yes." She had been angry at the time. Her father was missing, and Noah had just been taken by Umbra. That day couldn't be more than a week or two in the past. But it seemed like a lifetime ago.

"You've done a remarkable job of achieving your goal," said the agent. "Umbra's North American headquarters lies in ruins, and their power is greatly diminished. Unit 17 has suffered tremendous losses of both men and equipment. With your father, Noah, and the orb all lost, the problem of the spheres may go unsolved for centuries to come."

"But the cost of stopping them," whispered Harley. "The cost was terrible."

Cain nodded. "It always is." He slipped out the door and walked away along the beach.

To be continued . . .

ARCHWAY PAPERBACKS

EXTREME ZONE #4

PROOF OF PURCHASE OFFER

OFFICIAL RULES

1. To receive your free EXTREME ZONE baseball cap (approximate retail value: $8.00), submit this completed Official Entry Form and at least one Official Entry Form from either books 1, 2, or 3 (no copies allowed). Offer good only while supplies last. Allow 6-8 weeks for delivery. Send entries to the Archway Paperbacks/EZ Promotion, 13th Floor, 1230 Avenue of the Americas, NY, NY 10020.

2. The offer is open to residents of the U.S. and Canada. Void where prohibited. Employees of Simon & Schuster, Inc., its parent, subsidiaries, suppliers, affiliates, agencies, participating retailers, and their families living in the same household are not eligible. One EXTREME ZONE baseball cap per person. Ofier expires 12/31/97.

3. Not responsible for lost, late, postage due or misdirected responses. Requests not complying with all offer requirements will not be honored. Any fraudulent submission will be prosecuted to the fullest extent permitted by law.

EXTREME ZONE

Where your nightmares become reality

#1 Night Terrors
00241-4/$3.99

#2 Dark Lies
00242-2/$3.99

#3 Unseen Powers
00243-0/$3.99

#4 Deadly Secrets
00244-9/$3.99

visit the website at http://www.simonsays.com
coming soon

An Archway Paperback
Published by Pocket Books